NO END OF BLAME
Scenes of Overcoming

By the same author

Stage Plays

Cheek
No One Was Saved
Alpha Alpha
Edward, The Final Days
Stripwell
Claw
Fair Slaughter
The Love of a Good Man
That Good Between Us
The Hang of the Gaol
The Loud Boy's Life

T.V. Plays

Cows
Mutinies
Prowling Offensive
Conrod
Heroes of Labour
Russia
All Bleeding
Heaven

Radio Plays

One Afternoon on the 63rd Level of the North Face
   of the Pyramid of Cheops the Great
Henry V in Two Parts
Herman with Millie and Mick

PLAYSCRIPT 99

NO END OF BLAME

Scenes of Overcoming

Howard Barker

JOHN CALDER · LONDON
RIVERRUN PRESS · NEW YORK

iv

First published in Great Britian 1981 by
John Calder (Publishers) Ltd.,
18, Brewer Street,
London W1R 4AS.

and in the USA 1982 by
Riverrun Press Inc.,
Suite 814, 175 Fifth Avenue,
New York, NY 10010

All performing rights in this play are strictly reserved and
applications for performance should be made to:
Judy Daish Associates Ltd.,
122 Wigmore Street.
London W1H 9FE

No performance of this play may be given unless a licence has been obtained
prior to rehearsal.

British Library Cataloguing in Publication Data
Barker, Howard
No end of blame. — (Playscript series; 99)
I. Title
822'.914   PR6052.A6485

ISBN 0 7145 3912 0 paperbound

Typeset in 9/10 point Times by Ged Lennox Design, Cheltenham.
Printed by The Hillman Press, Frome and bound by W.H. Ware Ltd.,
Clevedon.

NO END OF BLAME
Scenes of Overcoming

No End of Blame was first performed by the Oxford Playhouse Company at the Oxford Playhouse on the 11th February 1981.

The cast were:

PEASANT WOMAN/ART STUDENT/ 4th COMRADE/2nd AIR WOMAN/ TEA LADY	Stephanie Fayerman
BELA VERACEK	Paul Freeman
GRIGOR GABOR	Allan Corduner
HUNGARIAN OFFICER/ANTHONY DIVER	Graham Lines
1st HUNGARIAN SOLDIER/ART STUDENT/5th COMRADE/ 1st AIRMAN/JOHN LOWRY/ 2nd MALE NURSE	Kevin Costello
2nd HUNGARIAN SOLDIER/ART STUDENT/3rd COMRADE/ 1st CUSTOMS OFFICER/3rd AIRMAN/ MIK/3rd MALE NURSE	David Cardy
1st RED SOLDIER/GPU MAN/ BOB STRINGER/1st MALE NURSE	Nigel Gregory
2nd RED SOLDIER/SOVIET GARDENER/2nd CUSTOMS OFFICER 4th AIRMAN/PC DOCKERILL	Roger Frost
3rd RED SOLDIER/1st COMRADE/ SIR HERBERT STRUBENZEE/ 2nd AIRMAN/PC HOOGSTRATEN	Arthur Cox
STELLA/1st AIRWOMAN/ DR GLASSON	Jan Chappell
ILONA/SECRETARY	Jane Bertish
2nd COMRADE/BILLWITZ/FRANK DEEDS/4th MALE NURSE	Peter Howell

Directed by Nicolas Kent
Set designed by Stephanie Howard
Bela's Cartoons by Gerald Scarfe
Grigor's Drawings by Clare Shenstone

ACT ONE

Scene One

A remote place in the Carpathian Mountains, 1918. A naked woman, her clothes round her ankles, an expression of terror on her face, stands rigid in the centre of the stage. A Hungarian soldier, ragged and unshaven, sits on the ground, a sketchbook open on his knees. Beside him, a rifle. He sketches feverishly.

Drawing: GRIGOR's *'Soldiers Bathing.'*

GRIGOR *(shouts).*   Come on! Where are you! Just look at her! Just look at her breasts! I love her breasts, they go — they're like — they're utterly — harmonious — they fall — they sag — not sag — sink — not sag or sink — they — CONCEDE — that's what they do — CONCEDE — they are completely harmonious with gravity — WHERE ARE YOU? They are in total sympathy with — *(The* WOMAN *grabs her clothes and tries to run away.* GRIGOR *leaps to his feet and grabs his rifle.)* Don't run away! *(She freezes. He drops the rifle, Goes back to sketching.)* She keeps trying to run away — I wish I spoke Roumanian, is it — I'd say, look, I'm an artist, I don't kill girls — not that she's a girl, she's a woman, thank God — I can't draw girls — I hate girls — there's no concession in their flesh — too much defiance — everything pokes upwards — nipples, tits, bum, — everything goes upwards — all aspiration, ugh —

She tries to escape again. He grabs the rifle.

GRIGOR.   Don't run away! *(She freezes.)* Sorry — sorry — *(He throws down the rifle, picks up his sketchpad again.)* Look at her buttocks — Bela, look at them — do look at them — see what I say — *(BELA comes in, holding a sketchbook limply in his hand. He also wears a threadbare tunic.)* the female body accepts — concedes to gravity — is in profoundly intimate relations with the earth — the curve, you see — the curve is the most perfect line — eliminates all tension — WHY DON'T YOU DRAW! No, I haven't got it — haven't got it — no — *(He tears off a sheet, starts another.)* I am so sick of drawing men — soldiers bathing — never again — I have eighteen books of soldiers bathing — eighteen! — in my pack *(He scuttles to a new position.)* there, you see — the essential female line — the curve — does not resist but — *(BELA moves closer to the woman.)* Bela — *(BELA is staring at her.)* Bela — you are in my view — *(He does not move.)* My fucking view!
BELA.   I want to kiss her.

GRIGOR.   DRAW! DRAW! *(BELA just stares)* All right, I'll move —
   (He shifts to another angle) there was a peasant woman in the institute
   — remember her — the model with the shoulders — oh, what
   shoulders — the same shoulders — they went — no, I haven't got it —
   (He tosses away another page.)
BELA.   I don't mean kiss.
GRIGOR.   The shoulders are the most expressive single element — in
   human anatomy — fact! *(BELA is taking off his tunic.)* Bela! What are
   you doing, Bela? Be — la!

*GRIGOR leaps to his feet, seizes BELA as he advances on the WOMAN.
They struggle.*

BELA.   IT'S A WOMAN! IT'S A WOMAN, ISN'T IT!
GRIGOR.   YOU'RE HURTING ME . . .
BELA.   LET GO! LET GO! *(The WOMAN draws up her clothes and
   hobbles away)* She's run away!

*GRIGOR releases BELA; goes to pursue, then turns back, picks up the
rifle.*

GRIGOR.   HEY! HEY! STOP! I'LL SHOOT! *(He aims it clumsily after
   her.)* BANG! BANG! *(Pause. He lets the rifle droop. She disappears.
   GRIGOR turns to his friend.)* LOST MY MODEL, FUCK YOU!
BELA. *(sitting on the ground, nursing his groin).*   Beg pardon. . . .
GRIGOR.   SHOULDN'T HAVE!
BELA. *(lying back, wearily).*   No. . . .
GRIGOR.   Shouldn't have. . . .

Pause. BELA is about to sit up.

BELA.   Grigor —
GRIGOR.   Don't move —

He picks up his sketch pad, begins drawing BELA who is naked.

BELA.   Grigor, we have just butchered two million Russians, a million
   Italians, half a million Poles, the same number of Roumanians, some
   Greeks, some French, a few thousand English, a division of Bulgarians
   by mistake, we have trod on babies' brains and caught our boots up in
   the entrails of old women, yesterday we ate our breakfast on a table
   made of half a man, Grigor, I do not understand a morality which says
   we have to draw a line at petty theft!
GRIGOR.   Theft?
BELA.   Theft, yes. Two minutes of herself, perhaps less. I know the
   argument, of course, the argument goes —
GRIGOR.   Keep still!
BELA.   Goes — what is the value of an inhibition if it collapses under
   strain of opportunity? That's the argument. Either it is incumbent on
   me not to rape women at all, or I should rape women under all
   circumstances. But that should equally apply to killing, shouldn't it?
   WHAT IN GOD'S NAME ARE WE DOING HERE? *(Pause.)* Did I

move? *(Pause. He lies back. Distant sounds of an artillery bombardment.)* There is another argument. A rather shoddy argument. But I'll put it all the same, shall I? *(GRIGOR is drawing.)* SHALL I?

GRIGOR.   Please.

BELA.   The other argument says, if I hadn't raped her someone else would. Someone less considerate. *(Pause.)*

GRIGOR.   A considerate rape. . . .

BELA.   Yes.

GRIGOR.   I'm not sure I understand that.

BELA.   Then you haven't been raped. The shoddiness of this argument lies in the fact that my having raped her considerately does not preclude her being raped inconsiderately by someone else, so the end result is she gets raped twice. It's a terrible argument you did well to ignore, Grigor, I can only say how greatly I approve your action, sticking your knee there, swiftly, expertly, disabling me in such a way as —

GRIGOR.   I'm sorry —

BELA.   No, no! I mean to say you are a moral hero, in the midst of all this sin and shame and human vileness, where we eat our breakfast off a man's divided trunk, to find an act of selfless purity is like —

GRIGOR.   You're mocking me —

BELA.   I'M NOT MOCKING YOU!

Pause.

GRIGOR.   You've moved.

BELA.   Because I would have done it, even so. *(He stares at him.)* MY BAD SELF.

Pause. GRIGOR closes the book, gets up. There is a loud cry off.

FIRST SOLDIER *(off stage).*   SOLDIER GOT NO CLOTHES ON!

A SOLDIER rushes on, bearing rifle and fixed bayonet. A second SOLDIER follows.

SECOND SOLDIER.   SOLDIER GOT NO CLOTHES ON!

They point their weapons at BELA.

FIRST SOLDIER.   Don't get up!

An OFFICER enters. The FIRST SOLDIER begins rummaging in GRIGOR's pack.

OFFICER.   Why are you naked? Are you homosexuals?

BELA and GRIGOR look at one another in bewilderment.

SECOND SOLDIER.   ANSWER! ARE YOU QUEERS?

OFFICER.   A soldier removes his uniform in the presence of the enemy for one of two reasons only. He is going to desert or he is homosexual.

SECOND SOLDIER.   ARE YOU QUEERS!

BELA *goes to get up.*

FIRST SOLDIER. DON'T MOVE!

OFFICER. What is your name and unit?

SECOND SOLDIER. QUICK!

GRIGOR. Gabor. 77th Regiment. Field Telegraph.

BELA. Veracek. 18th Brigade Telephonists.

OFFICER. Give in your paybooks.

SECOND SOLDIER. PAYBOOKS! QUICK!

OFFICER. The penalty for homosexuality is death, Field Punishment regulations. Are you guilty?

BELA/GRIGOR. No!

OFFICER. Then you were planning to desert.

BELA. No!

OFFICER. Then why throw your uniform away?

FIRST SOLDIER. Captain! *(He is holding* GRIGOR's *sketch pad.)* These books are full of naked men.

He shows them to the officer, who flicks through them with appreciation. FIRST SOLDIER *looks pruriently over his shoulder. The* OFFICER *snaps the last book shut.*

OFFICER. Thank God.

FIRST SOLDIER. Why?

OFFICER. He has seen fit to furnish us with proof — *(He turns to* BELA *and* GRIGOR.*)* On the authority invested in me by the Emperor Charles VIII, I sentence Privates — *(Pause, he looks at the* SECOND SOLDIER, *who is flicking through the sketchbooks.)* ON THE AUTHORITY INVESTED IN ME — *(The* SOLDIER *tosses down the books.)* by the Emperor Charles VIII, I sentence Privates —

SECOND SOLDIER *(looking at the paybooks).* Gabor —

OFFICER. Gabor —

SECOND SOLDIER. Veracek —

OFFICER. And Veracek to Field Punishment Class I.

GRIGOR. Bela —

FIRST SOLDIER. KNEEL!

GRIGOR. BE — LA!

OFFICER. In view of the present emergency and the threat to the territorial integrity of the Empire, the Chief Chaplain to the Army has declared all soldiers who die by summary execution may pass into the other world unshriven.

FIRST SOLDIER. KNEEL!

They kneel.

GRIGOR. BE — LA!

BELA. I took my clothes off because —

Pause.

GRIGOR. Tell them!

BELA.   Because I saw a woman.

Pause.

OFFICER.   You saw a woman. Do you always take your clothes off
  when you see a woman?
BELA.   I wanted to rape her.
OFFICER.   You undress to rape someone? What are you, a poet?
BELA.   Yes.

Pause.

OFFICER *(to* FIRST SOLDIER*).*   Tell the poet the penalty for rape.
FIRST SOLDIER.   FIELD PUNISHMENT CLASS 1.
OFFICER *(to* GRIGOR*).*   You. Over there.

GRIGOR *scrambles away. Leaving* BELA *alone on his knees.*

GRIGOR.   Tell him! Tell him she ran away!
OFFICER.   Take aim.

The SOLDIERS *rattle their bolts.*

GRIGOR.   SHE RAN AWAY!
OFFICER.   AIM!

They aim their rifles at BELA. *Pause.*

BELA.   Don't shoot me. The war's over.
OFFICER.   The war's over? The war's over, he says. What's that, then?

He cups his ear. Distant gunfire rumbles.

BELA.   We've lost.
OFFICER.   WE HAVE NOT LOST! WE HAVE NOT LOST AS
  LONG AS WE RESIST! *(Pause.* BELA *hangs his head. An
  unbearable delay. The* SOLDIERS *look at their* OFFICER.*)* Make up
  a poem.
BELA.   Wha'?
OFFICER.   A poem. Quick.
FIRST SOLDIER.   POEM! QUICK!

Pause. BELA *sweats.*

GRIGOR.   Bela . . . Bela . . . a poem. . . .
BELA.   ALL RIGHT —
GRIGOR.   Go on. . . .
OFFICER.   I have impeccable taste. I like above all, the heroic, national
  style. . . .
FIRST SOLDIER.   POEM, QUICK!

Pause.

BELA.   I drew my finger down his thigh . . .
     Laying my brown male hand upon his brown male breast . . .
GRIGOR.   BE — LA!

Pause.

BELA.   An insect lapped its moisture from his eye. . . .
   Blood quit his wound, coy as a girl leaving a bed. . . .

Pause, then with a groan he falls forward onto his hands.

OFFICER.   Breast and bed are not full rhymes. If you had said —
   forgive me — the blood in scarlet dressed — you see?
BELA.   That's better, yes.
OFFICER.   Much better.
BELA.   Yes.
OFFICER.   That would have rhymed.
BELA.   Yes.

Pause.

OFFICER.   I drew my finger down his thigh . . . you say it. . . .
BELA.   I drew my finger down his thigh. . . .
OFFICER.   Laying —
BELA.   Laying my brown male hand upon his brown male breast . . .
   An insect —
OFFICER.   Lapped —
BELA.   Lapped its moisture from his eye . . . Blood quit his wound —
   in scarlet dressed. . . .

Pause.

OFFICER.   It is better.
BELA.   Yes.
OFFICER.   I like rhyme. Poetry without rhyme is laying bricks without
   cement.

There is a fusilade of shots offstage.

SECOND SOLDIER.   COMM — UNISTS!

He throws away his rifle and rushes off.

OFFICER *(drawing his pistol.)*   Walk towards the shooting!

He goes off in the direction of the firing.

FIRST SOLDIER *(to BELA)*.   No 'ard feelings, mate?

He throws this weapon away and follows the SECOND SOLDIER off.
BELA remains on his knees. Sporadic shooting.

GRIGOR.   Bela . . . get up.
BELA.   I can't. . . .
GRIGOR *(pulling him)*.   Come on! Get up!
BELA.   I CAN'T GET UP.
GRIGOR.   Bela!
BELA.   I shall never write a poem again.
GRIGOR.   Never mind that now —
BELA.   NEVER AGAIN!

As GRIGOR *tugs at his arm,* RED SOLDIERS *come in, ragged armbands on their sleeves.*

FIRST RED SOLDIER.   War's over, boys. Go 'ome and fuck your wife.

BELA *falls against the man's knees.*

GRIGOR.   They were going to shoot us!
FIRST RED SOLDIER.   What for?
GRIGOR.   Because we —
BELA.   Nothing . . . nothing . . . shut up, Grigor. . . .
FIRST RED SOLDIER *(as the* OFFICER *is brought in).*   Shoot them now. *(He flings a rifle at* GRIGOR. *He catches it. A* SECOND RED SOLDIER *forces the* OFFICER *to the ground.* BELA *gets up).*
OFFICER.   I have a widowed mother. I am everything to her.
SECOND RED SOLDIER *(to* GRIGOR*).*   Bang away, mate.
OFFICER.   Couldn't you be satisfied with beating me? I ask because of my mother. She is a gracious lady, you would like her.
FIRST RED SOLDIER.   I got a mother, far from gracious. When she shouts the crockery spills in every kitchen in the street.
OFFICER.   Really?
FIRST RED SOLDIER.   And when she sits, her knees open like scissors. Most ungracious, she is. You would 'ate her.
OFFICER.   Me, I don't think I —
BELA.   GIVE ME THE RIFLE.

GRIGOR *looks at him in horror.*

BELA.   Give me the rifle.
GRIGOR.   Bela, you can't blame him!
BELA.   CAN'T BLAME HIM?
GRIGOR.   He was only — he was doing what —
BELA *(turning to the* OFFICER*).* He says I can't blame you. I DO BLAME YOU.
GRIGOR.   Bela, listen to me —
BELA.   HE HURT ME!
GRIGOR.   He hurt me too, but —
SECOND RED SOLDIER.   Buck up, will yer, Grig?
GRIGOR.   Think, please think — I CAN'T BEAR KILLING! DON'T! *(*SECOND RED SOLDIER *tosses* BELA *his rifle.)* NOW, LOOK!

With a yell BELA *drags the* OFFICER *off his knees and runs out with him.* GRIGOR *goes to follow but is blocked. Pause.*

FIRST RED SOLDIER.   Listen, Grig, there must be killing in this world, because we're angry, and we 'ave our rights. Anyone who tells you killing is just killing tells you lies. There is all the difference in the world between a rich man's and a poor man's death. You must know this, Grig, or we will never build a better world. . . .

There is a shot. The RED SOLDIERS *drift off. After a few moments,*

BELA *enters, the rifle limply in his hand.*

GRIGOR.   I can't ever be your friend. I'll walk with you, eat with you, but I shall never be your friend.

BELA.   Oh?

He puts down the rifle, picks up his tunic.

GRIGOR.   Although we'll talk, I'll tell you nothing. *(*BELA *puts the tunic on.)* Because friendship is nothing if it isn't pure. We were pure, and now we're not.

BELA.   He went on about rhyme. Fuck rhyme. I hate it.

GRIGOR.   I would have given anything to stay your friend —

BELA.   Balls to rhyme! Balls to the heroic, national style! His brains were pitiful, the pus of dead imagination on the ground, all his rhyming couplets running in the mud. . . .

GRIGOR.   Friendship dies, Bela —

BELA.   Fuck your friendship! Take your friendship back! I did what all my being told me to, cried out for, I was stifling, then I did it and I breathed! What do I care if your friendship draws its soft head in, all shocked and simpering? Keep your gift, I piss on it! *(He picks up his rucksack.* GRIGOR *crawls over the ground collecting his scattered drawings.* BELA *looks at him. Pause.)* I didn't shoot him, Grigor. I made him lie down and fired in the air. . . .

Pause, GRIGOR *looks joyous.*

GRIGOR.   Bela! Oh, Bela!

He goes to embrace him.

BELA.   Don't touch me! *(He stops.)* Don't celebrate the flinching of a coward. Don't kiss me because I drew back from a decent deed.

GRIGOR.   I'm sorry, Bela. . . .

BELA.   Let's go home. Four years of soldiering, and we never put a wound in anyone. . . .

They go off.

Blackout.

Scene Two

The life class at the Institute of Fine Art, Budapest. A female model sitting on a chair, surrounded by students, among them BELA *and* GRIGOR. BELA *still wears his army greatcoat. The silence of attentive work. It is 1921.*

Sketch: *'We will Revive the Spirit of Hungary.'* *Grotesque cartoon of two soldiers beating a man to death.*

STELLA *(at last)*. Christ, I am thin. *(Pause.)* Christ, I am. *(Pause.)* Before the war — may I speak — my knees — you should have seen 'em. *(Groan from somewhere.)* You groan, you never saw 'em. *(Pause.)* In silk. *(Groan again.)* In silk they were! *(Pause.)* They bloody were. *(Pause.)* Had hands all over 'em. *(Pause.)* Under tables. In the Cafe Esterhazy. *(Pause.)* The toast of Budapest. I quote. *(Pause.)* Had lawyers' fingers creeping over 'em. *(Pause.)* Tongues of magistrates went lick, lick, lick.

GRIGOR. You moved.

STELLA. Did I? Beg pardon. *(Pause.)* No, only saying the scrag was lovely once. Gave aches to princes while you played soldiers in the mud. *(Pause.)* Most fondled female in the Empire. *(Groans and laughter.)* Was! Was! Fact!

GRIGOR. Could you just keep your mouth —

STELLA. Look, Grig, I'm talking, darling —

GRIGOR. I know that, Stella —

STELLA. So how can I keep my mouth —

GRIGOR. It makes your head move —

STELLA. It would do, wouldn't it? *(Pause.)* Where was I?

GRIGOR. Oh, look —

BELA. Fondled.

STELLA. Fucked in fur, shagged in chiffon —

BELA. Sucked in silk!

Laughter.

GRIGOR. Look, this is supposed to be a life class!

STELLA. This is life, darling!

BELA. Sit down, Grigor!

STELLA. I haven't moved. Have I? I have not moved. *(Pause.)* Was kept in silk stockings by an army contractor who put paper soles on army boots. . . . *(Pause.)* I saw 'is body in the street. Flies running down 'is mouth, 'is mouth that used to suck my toes. . . . *(Pause.)* You've stopped drawing, Bela. Have you caught the magic of my knees?

BELA. They've lost something, Stella, through being wedged apart so much.

STELLA. They have. . . .

BELA. I wouldn't buy you a sausage sandwich for the joy of being there.

STELLA. Thank you! Likewise your little spurt of pleasure, dear.

GRIGOR *(jumping up again)*. CAN YOU KEEP STILL, PLEASE! You will keep talking and when you talk you get emotional! Emotion makes you move. It animates you, do you see? Why can't you just — it says on the instructions models are requested not to speak!

BELA. It animates you, Stella —

GRIGOR. We are here to study human form —

BELA.   Animates you, darling —

GRIGOR.   Oh, look, Bela —

BELA.   We do not want to hear the wreckage of your life, all right? Be a
form, Stella. Be art. Thank you! *(Pause. GRIGOR looks at BELA
coldly, sits again.)* There. Perfect form. No grievance. No sin. No spit.
No wit. No shit.

STELLA *bursts out laughing.*

GRIGOR   *(standing   again).*   YOU   ARE   DELIBERATELY
SABOTAGING THIS!

ILONA.   Grigor, they're laughing at you. Sit down, Grigor.

Pause, he sits.

STELLA.   I've had one good lover in my life. A sailor in the Red Guard.
I'll tell you this, and then shut up, all right, Grigor? He never said to
me — not once — I worship you. Never once called me 'is goddess. Or
'is angel. Never once. I said why don't you say you worship me? They
always did, the racketeers. I was their idol. He said, because I give you
dignity, my love. . . .

*Pause, suddenly she bursts out crying, covering her face with her hands.
The head of the Institute appears. Looks at her.*

BILLWITZ.   Stay like that. *(She sobs.)* Why aren't you drawing? Draw!
Draw! *(They begin sketching, feverishly. BELA does not move.
BILLWITZ moves round them.)* Why are we artists? We are artists
because we thrill to beauty. We look for beauty everywhere. In tears.
In pain. We need beauty now. Our hearts cry out. Who drew this
please? *(He holds out a paper, which is the cartoon 'We will Revive the
Spirit of Hungary'.)* When I see beauty mocked I flush with temper. I
tremble at the humiliation of my fellow man. Artists are the guardians
of beauty, high priests in the temple art. Who drew it? One of you did.
(No one replies. He walks round.) We suffer, oh, don't we suffer?
Little human creatures spilled and broken on howitzered hills and
maimed in gaols? We reconcile, we reconcile! No wonder I feel
anguish when my wounds are opened up again. Who did this please?

Pause.

BELA.   Me.

Pause.

BILLWITZ.   I knew you did. I knew my darling would hurt me most, my
best give me most pain. Everybody go now, please! Quick! But Bela.
God, I wish it had been someone else. *(The students leave, STELLA
puts on her gown. Goes out behind them. BELA stays sitting in his
chair. BILLWITZ walks up and down.)* It is not art.

BELA.   I feel it. So it is.

BILLWITZ.   It is not true. It is not half as true as any life drawing you
did for me.

BELA. It's more true.

BILLWITZ. It's prejudice!

BELA. It's more true than any painting you did in your life. Though it took me ten minutes, it's better than any canvas you pored over, sweated through, wept for, exhibited, took pride in, anything.

BILLWITZ. YOU WILL NEVER BE A GREAT PAINTER IF YOU DO NOT TELL THE TRUTH!

BELA. I don't want to be a painter. I hate oils, studios, manipulating colours inches thick. Give me ink, which dries quick, speaks quick, hurts.

BILLWITZ. Heal us, Bela. If there was ever a people needed healing, it is us. . . . (Pause. BELA does not move.) I have just come from the police.

BELA. MY ART SPEAKS, THEN! (He jumps up.) Did any single picture of yours win you such an accolade? A visit from the police! There is a diploma, there is a prize! Now I know I am a genius, now I hang in the echoing gallery of human art! I STIRRED THE POLICE, THEREFORE, I TOUCHED THE TRUTH. You make my case for me. . . . (Pause.) Will they beat me? I am terrified of being beaten. Will you keep them off me? You're famous, I'm not. . . .

Pause.

BILLWITZ. You have a terrible vanity Bela. . . .

BELA. Protect me, will you?

BILLWITZ. You are to be expelled.

BELA *looks up at him. A smile spreads over his face.*

BELA. Expelled? I thought they were going to hit me! (He laughs again.) Expelled! (He laughs.) Now I shall never learn to paint a nude, shall I? Never discover which corner of a corpse you put the legs! Or if a tit goes on the front or back? (Pause. He looks at BILLWITZ.) I leave Hungary. To policemen, bankers, swindlers, whores, English officers, French diplomats . . . and reconcilers painting peasants in the sun. (He goes near to BILLWITZ.) Kiss me, you old tragedy. . . .

BILLWITZ *kisses his cheek, goes out.* BELLA *closes his eyes, takes deep breaths.* GRIGOR *appears.*

GRIGOR. Bela? Bela?

BELA (turning boldly). They threw me out!

GRIGOR. Oh, God. . . .

BELA. ME! AND I AM THE BEST ARTIST OF THE LOT!

GRIGOR. Yes. . . .

BELA. Dead place, Grig! Stink of old corpse coming through national flag! Admiral's piss and papal vomit! The best Hungarians are dead. We have to leave, Grigor.

GRIGOR. What?

BELA. Shove off. (Pause. GRIGOR seems shaken.) Do you want to suffocate? Drown on a thimbleful of lies pissed out the bladder of a landscape painter? Death to the national fucking genius! Get your bag packed! Tell them you REJECT! *(Pause.)* What? *(Pause.)* Horrid silence. *(Pause.)* Horrid, dirtly little silence while the ego ticks. *(He cups his hand to his ear, mockingly.)* His calculator. Click! Brr! Brr! Brr! *(Angrily.)* WHAT! WHAT! `

GRIGOR.   I haven't yet completed one year of the course. . . .

BELA.   Stroke of luck.

GRIGOR.   Why?

BELA.   Poisoning not yet affected vital parts.

GRIGOR.   You see, I —

BELA.   OH, WHAT?

GRIGOR.   I wanted —

BELA.   A Diploma? Shabby bit of paper for performing dog?

GRIGOR.   LET ME SPEAK, WILL YOU! LET ME SPEAK! *(Pause. BELA sits down.)* I have been in a world war, in a civil war, in a revolution, in a counter-revolution, and I only want a little corner where I CAN PAINT. *(Pause.)* I live for it. Forgive pretentiousness of this, Bela, but actually, I live for it. The human form. Sorry about this. I have a passion for it. Sorry.

Pause.

BELA.   All the barrages we lay under . . . in our foxholes holding hands . . . digging one another out of human mess . . . pulled seven corpses off you once. Scooped guts out your mouth, wiped viscera out of your bulging eyes. . . .

GRIGOR.   Yes. . . .

BELA.   No Russian bombs could blow our promises apart. Takes peace to do that.

GRIGOR.   Listen —

BELA.   No! War is so childish! One says so many silly things with death next door! With death shoving its mouth against the sandbags, say a lot of babble, not from the head, just speaking from the bowels —

GRIGOR.   ALL RIGHT, I'LL COME!

Pause.

BELA.   Good. Go and tell him you resign. *(He jumps up.)* With sneers. With curling mouth issuing fine spray of contempt. Go on.

GRIGOR.   Now?

BELA.   Yes! Now, of course! While you're full of TEMPER. In his office. Fling your weight about! Shake the vases! Make the typist blush. I know you when you're wild. *(He smiles. GRIGOR starts to go out.)* Grig. *(He stops.)* Grig, I will find you nudes. Get nudes for you, anywhere.

GRIGOR.   Yes. . . .

BELA *(going to him).*   What is it you like? Their bums, is it? Makes you go —

He grabs GRIGOR by the crutch.

GRIGOR.   YOU MAKE ME VERY ANGRY.

Pause.

BELA *(walking away).* Yes. . . . *(GRIGOR leaves. The girl student ILONA comes in.)* I'm going, Ilona. No more life class for me. No more pencil and rubber, trying to get the setting of her poor old joints. Never did her justice, anyway. . . .

ILONA. Take me.

Pause.

BELA. No. You smell of Budapest. Rank with blood and coffee, fear and petits-fours. . . .

ILONA. Take me.

He stares at her, then suddenly extends his arm.

BELA. That way — Russia! *(He extends the other arm.)* That way — France! *(Pause, then with inspiration, hurries to the blackboard. He takes a piece of chalk and divides the board, writing 'Russia' in one column and 'France' in the other. He extends his arm again.)* That way —

Pause.

ILONA. Tolstoy!

BELA *puts one point under 'Russia'. Then extends his arm again.*

BELA. That way —
ILONA. Flaubert!

He ticks 'France' and so on. . . .

BELA. That way —
ILONA. Pushkin!
BELA. That way —
ILONA. Baudelaire!
BELA. That way —
ILONA. Mayakovsky!
BELA. That way —
ILONA. Appolinaire!
BELA. That way —
ILONA. Lenin!
BELA. That way — *(Pause.)* That way — *(Pause.)* That way —

She shrugs. He adds up the figures. Russia wins 4 - 3. He looks at her.

ILONA. Marry the future! Divorce the past! *(He smiles.)* I'll pack a bag.
BELA. No. Why pack a bag? A bag says, you came, so you can go back again. We don't go back again.
ILONA. Got no stockings. Bela, Russia's cold.

He goes to a desk, dips a paintbrush in some colour, goes to her. Kneels, and rapidly paints her legs. He stops.

BELA. Fuck. Laddered it.

Blackout.

Scene Three

The offices of the Writers' and Artists' Union, Moscow. A single table. People enter with chairs from various directions. Some have brief cases. It is 1925.

Sketch: 'The New Economic Plan'. A capitalist is robbing an old Bolshevik. The figure of Lenin, behind a wall, covers his eyes.

FIRST COMRADE. 'morning, Anatol.
SECOND COMRADE. I'll have that chair —
FIRST COMRADE. 'morning, I said —
SECOND COMRADE. Sorry, Roy —
FIRST COMRADE. S'all right, s'all right —
THIRD COMRADE. Roy, did you do that paper?
FIRST COMRADE. I did, I have it, I will give it to you —
THIRD COMRADE. Thank you.
FIRST COMRADE. 'ullo, Ludmilla —
THIRD COMRADE. I'll collect it off you afterwards, shall I?
FIRST COMRADE *(sitting, opening his bag)*. I love that skirt *(She ignores him.)* I do. I love that skirt. My wife wears such dismal skirts. Why is it? I dunno. Whenever you see Ludmilla she 'as —
SECOND COMRADE. Is everybody here yet?
FIFTH COMRADE. 'ello, 'ello, 'ello! Anyone got me a chair?
FIRST COMRADE. Certainly not. Get your own chair.
FIFTH COMRADE. The finest poet in the USSR and —
THIRD COMRADE. Opinion —
FIFTH COMRADE. An opinion, obviously — and I am reduced to transporting chairs —
FIRST COMRADE. Only your own chair, Oleg —
FIFTH COMRADE. Roy — no humour, love.

He goes out again.

THIRD COMRADE. Will somebody remind me, there is a meeting of the entertainments committee this afternoon? Everyone invited, needless to say.
FIRST COMRADE. Drinks?
THIRD COMRADE. Yes.
FIRST COMRADE. On the fund, though?
THIRD COMRADE. Yes, out the funds of course.

SECOND COMRADE *(at the table)*. I'd like to push on please, everyone.

FOURTH COMRADE. Yes, let's please.

FIFTH COMRADE. I wanted to sit next to Ludmilla.

FOURTH COMRADE. Why?

FIFTH COMRADE. Why, she says!

FIRST COMRADE. Oleg's a poet, that's why.

FOURTH COMRADE. I still don't see —

SECOND COMRADE. I take it everybody's read the papers on this one? Have they? Everybody?

THIRD COMRADE. On the train.

FIRST COMRADE. I have.

SECOND COMRADE. Shall we get him in, then? I take it he's here.

FIRST COMRADE. Who's introducing it?

FIFTH COMRADE. You are.

FIRST COMRADE. Get stuffed.

FOURTH COMRADE. Why not you?

FIRST COMRADE. Why not me?

FOURTH COMRADE. Yes, why not?

SECOND COMRADE. Because he always does it.

FIRST COMRADE. Thank you, Anatol. Someone notices. Someone appreciates.

SECOND COMRADE. What about you, Vasily?

THIRD COMRADE. Rather not.

FOURTH COMRADE. He never does, do you?

FIRST COMRADE. Well, have a go.

THIRD COMRADE. I'd rather not.

FIRST COMRADE. Well, I'm not doing it again! You do it, Anatol.

FOURTH COMRADE. Anatol is addressing the foreign correspondents this afternoon.

FIRST COMRADE. Of course, of course! And what about you, Oleg?

FIFTH COMRADE *(shakes his head)*. Sorry.

FIRST COMRADE. Not well enough briefed, I suppose?

FIFTH COMRADE. Exactly —

FIRST COMRADE. Oh, 'ere we go, all right, all right. Give in now, I may as well — I don't suppose you — *(He looks at FOURTH COMRADE, who shakes her head.)* No, I didn't think you would. All right.

FIFTH COMRADE. Hooray!

FIRST COMRADE. Lord High Executioner.

SECOND COMRADE. I don't think we should look at it like that.

FIRST COMRADE. Joke, Anatol.

FOURTH COMRADE. Jokes reveal attitudes.

FIRST COMRADE. Bloody 'ell —

FOURTH COMRADE. They do.

FIFTH COMRADE. Get on, shall we?

SECOND COMRADE. Ask him in, then.

FIFTH COMRADE *goes out of the room. The others read their papers.*
FIRST COMRADE *lights a cigarette.*

FIRST COMRADE.   Sorry, Ludmilla. Got to smoke.
SECOND COMRADE.   Vasily, would you fetch in another chair?
FOURTH COMRADE.   Have you had your child yet, Anatol?
SECOND COMRADE.   No.

THIRD COMRADE *goes out, returns with a chair.*

FOURTH COMRADE.   You want a boy I suppose?
SECOND COMRADE.   Not at all, Ludmilla, no.
THIRD COMRADE *(putting it in the middle).*   There?
SECOND COMRADE.   That's fine.

They read on. FIFTH COMRADE *appears with* BELA, *smiling and still wearing his army greatcoat.*

BELA.   Good morning.
ALL COMRADES.   Good morning — How do you do —

BELA *shakes hands with them all.*

FIRST COMRADE.   I know that coat.
SECOND COMRADE.   Would you care to take a chair?
BELA.   Here?
SECOND COMRADE.   Thank you, yes.
FIRST COMRADE *(still standing).*   I know that coat.
BELA.   It's a little bit the worse for wear. All the best wool went to
   make the officers' bed rolls.
FIRST COMRADE.   Infantry. Hungarian Infantry.
BELA.   Telegraphy.
FIRST COMRADE *(sitting).*   I knew it. Had a brush with you at
   Przemysl.
BELA.   Not me, I think.
FIRST COMRADE.   You weren't at Przemysl?
BELA *(affably).*   No, and even if I had been, I shouldn't have brushed
   with you. I never brushed with anyone.
FIRST COMRADE.   Me neither. Figure of speech. We love your work,
   comrade.
BERLA.   Thank you.
FIFTH COMRADE.   The best.
BELA.   Thank you.
FIRST COMRADE.   So I'll begin by saying no one here — or anywhere
   else for that matter — disputes your talent.
FIFTH COMRADE.   You are a master.
BELA.   Oh. . . .

FIRST COMRADE *flicks through sheaf of drawings.*

FIRST COMRADE.   Incredible. *(And on.)* Lovely *(He shows it to*
   FOURTH COMRADE.*)* Look at that.

He shakes his head.

FOURTH COMRADE *(leaning over).* Yes. . . .

FIRST COMRADE. Wonderful. I'll tell you something about that one —

He holds it up.

SECOND COMRADE. Yes, do tell him.

FIRST COMRADE. No, you tell him, Anatol. I wasn't there.

SECOND COMRADE. Lenin was Guest of Honour at the annual conference of the Union of Printing and Graphic Trades in August, and he drew attention to your work.

FIRST COMRADE. Well, go on.

SECOND COMRADE. Praised it very highly.

FIRST COMRADE. No, Anatol will put things in the baldest manner possible — what Lenin said was —

SECOND COMRADE. You tell it —

FIRST COMRADE. He said why is there no one in the whole of the Soviet Union can draw half as well as this Hungarian chap? That's what he said.

SECOND COMRADE. Half as well.

FOURTH COMRADE. Lenin holds cartoons in the highest regard.

THIRD COMRADE. Yes.

FIRST COMRADE. So there we are. You can't do better than that. So anything we have to say, you interpret in the light of that, all right? Do you smoke? *(FIRST COMRADE chucks the packet.)* No, we're all fans here. To a man. Or to a woman. All right, Ludmilla? To a woman. *(She grimaces.)* I think I'd like to start by saying — as is my wont — that we are struggling — *(He stops.)* I 'ate struggling — we are trying, quite simply, trying — to evolve a different sort of art here. All right? An art which is not bourgeois. That is why you came here. Correct me if I'm wrong. That is why you came to Russia in the first place. Because although we have no shoe laces for our boots and no lenses for our spectacles, our art is free. By free I mean free of bourgeois constraints. By bourgeois constraints I mean the tying of the creative act to the demands of private ego. Individualism, I mean, all right? How am I doing?

BELA. All right.

FIRST COMRADE. Good. And it's not been easy, you know that. Everyone in this room has suffered in some way from trying, this particular type of trying. It has cost us, hasn't it? Given us trouble, and pain. A great deal of pain. But we believe it's worth it. And one of the ways we have continued, have kept up the struggle — why do I keep saying struggle, Anatol? I must get shot of struggle — one of the ways we have — sustained our effort — is through meetings like this, in which — sometimes happy, sometimes sad — we have exerted our communal will to rescue artists from their bourgeois habit. There. Have I put it fairly? Vasily?

THIRD COMRADE. I think so, yes.

SECOND COMRADE.   Good, Roy.

FIRST COMRADE.   Thank you. I get so much experience, you see. None of this lot will make the opening speech. Terrible, ain't it? I shall end up smooth and oily.

FIFTH COMRADE.   That'll be the day.

FIRST COMRADE.   So we ask you along, as a member of the Cultural Union because — why? Because — there is a feeling — a more or less unanimous feeling — that you — might benefit from a session of this sort. *(Pause.)* Voila! Now you say something. Fuck off, if you like.

He takes a drink of water from the table. BELA *is silent.*

FOURTH COMRADE.   Some people, you see, resist this very strongly. They think we are taking a liberty with their God-given right to speak their minds. They feel affronted. That is a negative response. We're not bureaucrats. You know Anatol. Vasily is a painter. Roy's a first rate critic. I'm a graphic artist. Oleg's a poet and a sculptor. You know that, you know that artists grow enormously when they exchange ideas. Take insights from each other. That's very good. A lonely artist withers, rots, dries up. We want to stimulate you. We are not bourgeois critics who see their role as destruction in the interests of maintaining existing cultural values. We attack existing cultural values. Am I going on too much?

FIRST COMRADE.   No, that's all good stuff, Ludmilla.

FOURTH COMRADE.   Yes, but does he understand it? *(Pause.)* I know a lot of artists have gone away from these meetings arguing with themselves, forced to confront things they had been hiding from. On your own, you can hide from anything can't you? And they became better artists. Even artists who were very good in the first place.

SECOND COMRADE.   I did.

FOURTH COMRADE.   Anatol is one.

SECOND COMRADE.   I was outraged. Everything in me prickled. I remember feeling terribly hot, and ashamed. But that was silly. Because I am an artist does not mean I'm not human, that I'm above criticism. But it must be the right criticism. With the right criticism I could benefit.

FIRST COMRADE.   Anatol's work has improved ten fold.

SECOND COMRADE.   Well, I don't know about ten fold —

FIRST COMRADE.   Ten fold.

Pause.

FOURTH COMRADE.   Do you want to speak?

Pause.

BELA.   Are you telling me I've done wrong?

FIRST COMRADE.   No. Let's get the word wrong disposed of, shall we? Chuck wrong out. The word wrong is —

FIFTH COMRADE.   Wrong.

FIRST COMRADE.   Thank you. In a sense, Bela, no artist can be wrong. I will be accused of residual bourgeois thinking — lovely phrase —

FOURTH COMRADE. You will —

FIRST COMRADE. Here we go — if I say no artist can be wrong — in the most fundamental sense — because he is obeying an impulse from somewhere within —

FOURTH COMRADE. I don't go along with this —

THIRD COMRADE. Me neither —

FIRST COMRADE. They don't go along with it —

FOURTH COMRADE. Absolutely not —

FIRST COMRADE. There you are, residual bourgois habit —

FOURTH COMRADE. Of course an artist can be wrong —

FIFTH COMRADE. Scrap it, Roy —

FIRST COMRADE. No. I won't entirely scrap it, I'll refine it —

FIFTH COMRADE. Scrap it!

FOURTH COMRADE. It's confusing him.

FIFTH COMRADE. It's confusing us —

FOURTH COMRADE. Yes.

FIRST COMRADE. Beg pardon, beg pardon, see I can't always be right —

FOURTH COMRADE. You damn well can't.

FIRST COMRADE. No artist does wrong knowingly. Or else he's not an artist. *(Pause. He cups his ear.)* Anyone?

FOURTH COMRADE. I don't understand it.

FIRST COMRADE. Oh, come on —

FOURTH COMRADE. I do not understand it.

FIRST COMRADE. Tell you later. You know what I mean, Bela, do you?

BELA. Yes.

FIRST COMRADE. But he can do wrong unknowingly. Because he has power. Artists are very dangerous people. That is why they go to prison, that is why they have gags stuck on their mouths. They are more dangerous than tanks and planes. It's a terrible power, this power of addressing hearts and minds, articulating the unspoken will of peoples. What a treasure that is, Bela, a gift of the most massive kind, a power which in the case of the very greatest artists, may be beyond even the control of genius itself. . . . *(Silence. He takes a drink.)* So. To this cartoon. *(He shuffles his papers. The others do the same. Noise of papers.)* Where is it? *(Rustling papers.)* Too much bloody paperwork.

FOURTH COMRADE. You are just untidy.

FIRST COMRADE. I am untidy, but there's still too much paperwork. Really, Anatol, can we cut down on this? *(He finds what he wants, stands, hands a copy to BELA.)* Do you want to comment on that cartoon?

(Pause. They all look at him.)

BELA. It's a very good example of my work.

FIRST COMRADE. Yes.

Pause.

BELA.   It's a superb piece of draughtsmanship.
FIRST COMRADE.   Yes. It is.

FOURTH COMRADE *looks at* THIRD. *Pause.*

BELA.   It's a bit too heavily shaded.
FIRST COMRADE.   Well, that's a matter of opinion.
BELA.   Quite.

Pause. FIRST COMRADE *takes his glasses off, rubs his eyes, replaces them.*

FIRST COMRADE.   Anything else? *(Pause.)* Oh, dear. . . .
SECOND COMRADE.   I don't think it will help much if you adopt a
     posture — if you — on principle resist what we are saying. Because it
     isn't really a very worthy principle, is it? If you think about it.
BELA.   I'm sorry —
SECOND COMRADE.   I think there's only one principle that we ought
     to be rigid about, and that is — do we, as artists, serve the people?
     That's the only one, I think.
BELA.   Yes.
SECOND COMRADE.   You agree with that?
BELA.   Yes.

FIRST COMRADE *lets out a sigh of relief.*

FOURTH COMRADE *(turning to him angrily).*   It's quite obvious he
     believes that! Don't insult him! Would he be here if he didn't believe
     that?
SECOND COMRADE.   I just wanted to clarify —
FOURTH COMRADE.   He doesn't need to clarify it. All these pictures
     clarify it.
SECOND COMRADE.   Obviously.

Pause.

FIRST COMRADE.   Yes. Which brings us to the tricky question,
     doesn't it? *(He draws breath.)* Is this cartoon saying — no — start again
     — Is what the cartoon says — in the service of the people? In other
     words, with reference to the criteria we have established and agreed
     upon — is it a good cartoon?

He looks around.

FOURTH COMRADE.   No.
SECOND COMRADE.   No.
FIFTH COMRADE.   Absolutely not.
BELA.   What is this? Are we counting heads?
FIRST COMRADE.   No, it was rhetorical question. Give us a fag.
     (BELA tosses him the packet.) Anybody else want to speak? I've done
     a lengthy introduction. *(Pause.)* Anyone?
SECOND COMRADE.   You go on.

FOURTH COMRADE.   You're doing very well.
FIRST COMRADE.   Never have the gift of the gab. Have you got the gift of the gab, Bela?
BELA.   No.
FIRST COMRADE.   Lucky feller. It's an almighty handicap.
FOURTH COMRADE.   Just go on.

Pause. FIRST COMRADE *drinks again.*

FIRST COMRADE.   In this cartoon — and others — there is a tendency — a critical tendency —
BELA.   It's a cartoon —
FIRST COMRADE.   Quite, it's a cartoon —
BELA.   Isn't a cartoon meant to be —
FOURTH COMRADE.   Let Roy finish —
FIRST COMRADE.   A tendency to criticize the line that Comrade Lenin is advancing. Which is — which is — unhelpful —
BELA.   Unhelpful?
FIRST COMRADE.   Let me go on a minute — not because Lenin is a god, not because he is infallible but because the experiment we are undertaking here, which drew you here in the beginning, which brought you and many others scuttling across the border, without a suitcase even I believe — this great experiment — must be endorsed by all the people, and not undermined. I mean, there is a case for criticism, but it's not now.

Pause.

SECOND COMRADE.   Would you care to reply to that?
BELA.   I did not scuttle across the border, I walked.
FIRST COMRADE.   Beg pardon.
BELA.   I did not bring a suitcase because I came to make Russia my home. And I came to make it my home because it's free.
FIFTH COMRADE.   Quite.
FOURTH COMRADE.   Good.
BELA.   Because to an artist, freedom of expression matters even more than nationality. I say that as a patriotic person, a person who loves his country and his people. Not as a licker of governments. I say it as a person who loves socialism and materialism. As a person who admires Lenin more than any other man alive. But to an artist freedom comes above all things, above —
SECOND COMRADE.   Wait a minute, wait a minute. Not above justice, surely? *(Pause. BELA is silent.)* You see, this is what we mean when we say we are against the bourgeois definition of an artist. We say an artist is only free if his society is free. He cannot be free AGAINST the freedom of his society. Can he? That is intellectual sickness. *(Pause.)* Isn't it?

Pause. BELA *stares ahead.*

BELA.   I am not a good intellectual.

FOURTH COMRADE.   You mustn't say that.
BELA.   I don't think I —
FOURTH COMRADE.   You mustn't shelter behind a fog of anti-intellectualism. That is a posture, a calamitous affectation, isn't it?
FIFTH COMRADE.   Carry on, Bela.

Pause. He seems unable to speak.

BELA.   It's oppressive in here, all this —
SECOND COMRADE.   It can seem oppressive, I agree —
FOURTH COMRADE.   It's not oppressive. It is not a persecution. We aren't the inquisition, are we? This is not the middle ages. Argue with us, please.

Pause.

SECOND COMRADE.   Yes. Defend your cartoon, please.

BELA *shuts his eyes.*

BELA.   There's something wrong somewhere.
SECOND COMRADE.   Where? Tell us where. *(Pause.)* Fight for your work. It won't speak for itself.
BELA.   It should do!
SECOND COMRADE.   But it won't
FIRST COMRADE.   Shall I get us all a cup of tea?
FOURTH COMRADE.   No, Roy, don't lighten the atmosphere. Bela is not a child, is he? He is a great artist.

FIRST COMRADE *gets up, walks a little.*

BELA.   I disagree with Lenin.
FIFTH COMRADE.   That is a supremely arrogant statement.
FOURTH COMRADE.   Of course it's not!
FIFTH COMRADE.   She says it's not.
FOURTH COMRADE.   He is entitled to disagree with anyone he wants. That's freedom, isn't it? But he must be able to restrain his criticism in the wider interests of the people. That's responsibility, isn't it?

Pause.

BELA.   So you are saying —
FIRST COMRADE.   Lenin sees much further than we do.
BELA.   Ah.
FIRST COMRADE.   And even if he didn't, we should have to follow him, because to resist him is to resist the revolution, isn't it? AT THIS TIME. *(Pause.)* Later on, yes, let's all squeal at once.
BELA.   BUT I WANT TO PROTEST!
FIRST COMRADE.   Tomorrow.

Pause.

BELA.   You have created a most terrible effect, quite unintentionally, the terrible effect of making me, who is so small and insignificant, a hero, a colossus towering over you, you who are so much better men than me, you shovel earth beneath my feet, and raise me up and up, aren't I vain enough already but you want to make me a saint, I who did so little, who have so little honour, AM MUCH GREATER THAN YOU! *(Pause.)* You should not do that. It makes me ashamed. . . .

Pause.

FOURTH COMRADE.   Bela, we stretch our little fingers out, to try to catch the swinging boot of history, treading generation after generation into blood, help us catch it, bend it, make it our tame thing. . . .

Pause. He tears up his cartoon, drops it on the floor. FIFTH COMRADE goes to him, embraces him. Scraping of chairs as the meeting breaks up.

FIRST COMRADE.   Anybody going my way?
THIRD COMRADE.   I better take that paper, Roy, while I remember.
FIRST COMRADE.   Anyone getting a bus? Oh, good —
FIFTH COMRADE *(calling as he leaves).*   Ludmilla, Ludmilla!

Blackout and instant silence.

Scene Four

A garden in a suburb of Moscow. A massive bed of flowers featuring a hammer and sickle. An old GARDENER is at work with a trowel. It is 1934. ILONA enters pushing a pram.

Drawing: GRIGOR'S *'Naked Woman Looking at her Feet.'*

GARDENER *(springing up, pointing with trowel).*   Geraniums — the blood of Russia — Chrysanthemums — the future of mankind — Lobelia — the solidarity of the party — Lily — Comrade Stalin's favourite plant. *(He stands to attention.)* Floral tribute of the 9th District Workers' Flats! *(He smiles, looks at the baby, kneels down again to work. BELA comes in, overcoated though it's a summer's day, with GRIGOR. The GARDENER leaps to his feet again.)* Geraniums — the blood of Russia — Chrysanthemums — the future of mankind — Lobelia — the solidarity of the party — Lily — Comrade Stalin's favourite plant. *(He stands to attention.)* Floral tribute of 9th District Workers' Flats!

He kneels down again.

ILONA.   I am perfectly prepared to have a child by each of you.
BELA.   Grigor isn't. Grigor doesn't fancy that.

GRIGOR.   I love her.

BELA.   So you keep saying.

ILONA.   It's been done before.

BELA.   Grigor thinks passion is exclusive. Grigor thinks passion's got
rights.

GRIGOR.   It has got rights!

BELA.   There you are. The gospel according to Saint Grigor. Flesh and
babies. Babies and flesh.

GRIGOR.   Can I speak for myself?

BELA.   Go ahead!

Pause.

GRIGOR.   We should go away. We have had twelve years of Moscow.
We should live in the forest.

BELA.   Oh, my God. . . .

GRIGOR.   We should expose ourselves unhesitatingly to our human
essence.

BELA.   Eat berries. Wipe our bums on leaves.

GRIGOR.   DON'T LAUGH AT ME! WHY DO YOU HAVE TO
LAUGH AT ME!

ILONA.   I can't live in the woods.

GRIGOR.   You love me. I love you.

ILONA.   Yes, but I can't live in the woods.

BELA.   Grigor thinks, because he is in love, that puts a stop to the
argument. You are in love — ergo — the woods!

GRIGOR.   Yes.

ILONA.   Grigor, I am secretary of the Works Committee.

GRIGOR.   That's not a reason for, or against, doing anything.

ILONA.   Of course it is.

BELA.   The truth about human nature, Grigor, is not lying underneath
an oak tree. I have sat under oak trees, and it isn't there.

GRIGOR.   Nobody wants to listen to me! Everybody wants to talk and
nobody wants to listen! Everybody wants to be clever and nobody
wants to be wise!

A MAN enters. He is a member of the GPU.

GARDENER *(leaping up)*.   Geraniums — the blood of Russia —
Chrysanthemums — the future of mankind — Lobelia — the solidarity
of —

GPU MAN.   Shut up.

*He shows briefly, a very small card. The GARDENER goes back to his
work.*

BELA *(deliberately)*.   I believe, historically speaking, the option of the
woods — the woods option, we'll call it — has been tried before. I
believe from time to time, at moments of crisis, at moments of doubt,
persons of a philosophic disposition have retreated to the relatively
unspoiled regions of the earth in search of wisdom, invariably in the
company of women with big tits —

GRIGOR.   Look, Bela, will you —

BELA.   But I don't believe, in all honesty, given the complexity of the present social and industrial machine, the woods option is a wholly satisfactory response, since the deliberate rejection of experience contributes nothing to the alleviation of human pain, nor relieves you from its consequences, or to put it brutally — *(He goes up to the* GPU MAN*)* You don't miss the bullets by shutting your eyes! *(Pause, smiles.)* Good morning. I thought we'd lost you on the underground.

ILONA.   Grigor, what are you looking for?

GRIGOR *shrugs.*

BELA.   I must say, Grigor's deceit is practically insupportable. All these years he has been consuming — ostensibly for artistic reasons — the nakedness of — dare I say, my wife? — his charcoal scratching white paper which his fantasy converted into bedroom sheets —

ILONA.   Shut up —

BELA.   When all the time, his intentions, conscious or unconscious, have been — I can hardly bring myself to say it!

ILONA.   Shut up —

BELA.   As if Moscow wasn't full of models! Splendid Russian women perfectly buttocked, gorgeous hipped! And he — in twelve years — has not attempted one! I should have seen it, a man with half my sensitivity would have known.

ILONA.   You do not love me. So you didn't know.

BELA.   She says I do not love her! And what's her evidence? That I trust her with my friend!

ILONA.   You know you don't.

BELA.   The absence of jealousy is perfect proof! God help us!

ILONA.   I SAID YOU KNOW YOU DON'T.

Pause.

BELA.   No. You're quite right. I'm not in love with you. *(Pause.)* Strange, how those words set you free. . . . *(Pause.)* Go to the woods if you want to. If they'll let you. Go.

GRIGOR.   You don't mind?

BELA.   Mind? Why should I mind? You exercise your will to oblivion, if it's oblivion you want. If the world hurts you, do it, bend your knee to mystery, drink dirty water, worship funny, little forest gods, dig out a religion for yourself.

GRIGOR.   I don't want a religion!

BELA.   You will have to have one! Go backwards and you must take the backwardness that goes with it. Make her your idol if you like. Her parts, her fecund this, her fertile that. Go down on your knees and lick her, offer up dead lambs on the altar of her magic cunt, carve women with huge bellies and tiny, rudimentary heads —

GRIGOR.   You don't know what —

BELA.   I do know! I know where the real fight is! It is against worship, it's against the surrender of your self! *(Pause.)* Will you wear clothes, or not? I see you in a tutu, sewn together from pigs' ears. . . .

ILONA.   Nobody asks me what I want. *(Pause.)* NOBODY ASKS ME WHAT I WANT.

BELA.   Ilona is getting emotional. *(Suddenly she weeps, covers her face bitterly.)* You see?

GRIGOR.   Don't cry. I cannot bear to see you cry.

BELA.   Let her.

GRIGOR.   I love you! Don't cry!

BELA *(shakes his head).*   Oh, Grigor . . . as if that could make her stop! Your little sticky thing of love! Your glue! Her head splits and he offers his smelly little tube of glue.

GRIGOR.   YOU DON'T KNOW HOW I HATE YOU SOMETIMES!

BELA.   You don't know how I hate myself.

Pause.

ILONA.   Sometimes, I really want to be myself. Want utter hardness. Be like a pebble, round and safe, and walk along a street, not going from anybody, nor to anybody. Whole. *(Pause.)* And then, when I feel most like that, stop dead suddenly, go cold and hot, and crumble, and pray somebody wants me, for anything, a fuck, a fingering, because it wants my milk or is afraid of the dark. *(Pause.)* And I go from one to the other, being ashamed or angry. I want to go to the woods, and I don't. I like being Grigor's goddess, and I don't. . . .

Pause.

GPU MAN.   Women . . . don't know what they do want. . . .

BELA.   And do you, comrade?

GPU MAN.   Me, comrade?

BELA.   Yes, comrade. Tell us what you want, comrade.

GPU MAN.   Think you caught me?

BELA.   No.

GPU MAN.   Yes, you do. *(Pause.)* I want Comrade Stalin to enjoy another forty years of health.

Pause. BELA *turns to* ILONA.

BELA.   It's my child in the pram, I believe. . . .

ILONA.   She stays with me.

He goes. Looks in the pram.

GRIGOR.   Come with us, Bela. . . .

BELA *(shakes his head).*   The quiet would kill me. Since they built it, I've done nothing but ride around the underground. . . . *(He picks the baby out, holds it up.)* Oh, Judith, don't let them fool you with their gods. . . .

GRIGOR.   WHAT ABOUT YOUR GODS! AREN'T THESE GODS!

He looks at the GPU MAN.

BELA *(putting the baby back).*   Send me drawings, will you? Of her growing up?

Pause. GRIGOR *hugs him tightly, then leaves with* ILONA. BELA *watches them disappear. Pause. The* GPU MAN *comes forward.*

GPU MAN.   Intellectuals. . . ! What does it matter what they say? *(Pause.)* Ask me, has industrial production risen much? *(Pause.)* Go on, ask me. *(Pause.)* ASK ME, THEN!

BELA.   Has industrial production risen much?

GPU MAN.   Rolled steel bars, seven hundred and fifty-eight per cent. Railway wagons, four hundred and twenty-six per cent. Chemicals, not including fertilizers, two hundred and seventeen per cent. Fertilizers, four hundred and one per cent. *(Pause.)* Ask me about housing now.

Pause.

BELA.   Housing, please.

GPU MAN.   Units of accommodation, six hundred and ninety-two per cent. *(Pause.)* Imagine all that happiness.

BELA.   Yes.

GPU MAN.   Comrade Stalin. People will talk about him for thousands of years. At night, I read those figures before I go to bed. That's how I live with pain, comrade.

Pause, BELA *moves away to leave. The* GARDENER *jumps up, eagerly.*

GARDENER.   Geraniums — the blood of Russia — Chrysanthemums — the future of mankind — Lobelia — the soldiarity of the party — Lily — Comrade Stalin's favourite plant. *(He stands to attention.)* Floral tribute of the 9th District Workers' Flats!

BELA *stares at the flowers. Suddenly he lets out a cry and plunges into the middle of the flower bed.*

BELA *(lying and writhing).*   IDOL — ATORY! IDOL — ATORY!

GARDENER *(in disbelief).*   Hey, you bugger! Out of there!

BELA.   IDOL — ATORY! IDOL — ATORY!

GARDENER.   That's art! That's my art you're rollin' on!

The GPU MAN *puts a whistle to his lips and blows loudly. Blackout.*

Scene Five

BELA *is standing holding a suitcase. He faces* FOURTH COMRADE *across the stage. They are isolated by spots.*

FOURTH COMRADE.   I put eye-shadow on. I put lip-colour on. I shopped for underwear. I found some which made me feel bridal, do you know what I mean? And new stockings, which I rolled up my

smooth legs, and in the car kept looking at them, at my perfect
untouched knees, and they were shaking. . . . *(Pause.)* And in the
Kremlin, going down the corridors, was thinking all the time, are my
seams straight . . . will someone tell me if my legs look nice, and from
the way they looked, the men who took my papers, who smelled me,
caught my scent of fear and roses, watched my trembling body pass
them, yes, knew I was nice, luscious with nerves and moistened lips,
and when the door behind the door after the door was opened, stood
there, saw him and —

BELA.   WHAT ABOUT ME!

She shuts her eyes. Pause.

FOURTH COMRADE.   Pissed myself. . . .

She shudders.

BELA.   Please, Ludmilla, what about me?

FOURTH COMRADE.   I said you had a momentary onset of dementia,
brought on by your wife's desertion. I think I said that. I may not have
done. To which he said, socialism had not yet discovered the answer to
domestic incompatability. I think he said that. I may have imagined it.
I wonder if he is immune to the stealthy smell of urine?

BELA.   But I am —

FOURTH COMRADE.   He wants you to have a holiday.

BELA *(horrified)*.   A holiday. . . !

Pause.

FOURTH COMRADE.   Visit relatives abroad.

Pause. He holds out the suitcase.

BELA.   I shan't be wanting this —

FOURTH COMRADE.   Take it. It means you may come back again.
(His hand drops. He goes to take a step towards her.) No, don't kiss me
goodbye. It will look as though I defended you for personal reasons.

BELA.   Would you like to kiss me?

FOURTH COMRADE.   Ideally, yes.

BELA.   May I imagine it?

FOURTH COMRADE.   Yes.

BELA.   Where?

FOURTH COMRADE.   On your lips.

BELA.   And you'll imagine mine, will you?

FOURTH COMRADE.   I will imagine yours.

BELA.   On your breasts?

FOURTH COMRADE.   If you say so. *(Pause. He smiles.)*Quick! Hurry
up!

The spots go out.

Scene Six

Dover, the Customs shed. A woman's voice over a tannoy announces a train departure. Two CUSTOMS OFFICERS *stand in a posture of lethargy against a desk.* BELA *enters, with suitcase. He kneels, kisses the ground.*

Sketch: *'The Dark Ages.' A Hitlerine bat, its wings outspread, casts a shadow over the European portion of the globe.*

FIRST OFFICER.   Oi! *(*BELA *kisses on.)* Oi! Cut that out.

He walks over, lazily.

BELA.   I kiss this soil, I kiss this ground. I kiss. I kiss.
SECOND OFFICER.   'ave that bag over 'ere, please!
BELA *(grasping the officer's ankles).*   Kiss this trouser! Kiss this feet!
FIRST OFFICER.   Mind my creases!
SECOND OFFICER.   That bag over 'ere, please!
FIRST OFFICER.   GET YOUR FINGERS OFF MY CREASE! *(Pointing to the suitcase).* On the desk.
BELA *(standing, holding out his suitcase).*   Nothing!
SECOND OFFICER.   That's what you say.
BELA.   Emptiness!
SECOND OFFICER.   That's what you say, is it?

BELA *puts it down. The* SECOND OFFICER *snaps open the locks.*

SECOND OFFICER.   Fuckin' is, an' all.
BELA.   I got nothin'! Only freeness! Breathe it, see? No magic here!
FIRST OFFICER.   Got nothing, eh?
BELA.   Nothin'!

He grins.

FIRST OFFICER.   You may not enter the territories of His Britannic Majesty without the equivalent in currency of ten pounds —
BELA.   It rains on me, I don't care! I lie under hedges and the rain piss on me, who cares? I am empty belly, I DO NOT CARE, I am rich, see, I am dressed in freeness, I am eating freeness, see?
FIRST OFFICER.   dom.
BELA.   Beg pardon?
FIRST OFFICER.   dom. Not ness.
SECOND OFFICER.   Have you the equivalent of ten pounds?
BELA.   No money.
FIRST OFFICER.   Right.
BELA.   Got this — *(He takes out a pencil)* Draw your picture. Beautiful English face —
FIRST OFFICER.   Come on —
BELA *(inhaling).*   I breathe, see, breathe deep of English wind!
FIRST OFFICER *(to* SECOND OFFICER*).*   Michael! Get this silly bugger out of here!

A man enters from the opposite direction. He greets BELA.

STRUBENZEE.   Mr Veracek? I'm Sir Herbert Strubenzee, *(He holds out a hand.* BELA *grasps it. Falls to his knees.)* No, no, you don't kneel to me, I am a knight but you still don't have to. . . . We pride ourselves on being rather casual about things like rank — *(He turns angrily to* OFFICERS.*)* DON'T LAUGH AT HIM, PLEASE! *(Turns back to* BELA *who gets up.)* Welcome to Great Britain, *(To* FIRST OFFICER.*)* Take his case.

BELA.   No, no, I take my —

STURBENZEE.   He likes taking cases. I say, what a spiffing coat!

BELA *stops, looks down at the greatcoat, then unbuttons it, and takes it off. He looks at it, drops it on the floor. They go out.* SECOND OFFICER, *with studied casualness, walks over, a clipboard in one hand. With the other, using two fingers, he plucks it up. Suddenly, the violent interruption of sound effects: The monotonous firing of a light gun,* ILONA'S *voice desperately calling for* GRIGOR. *The* SECOND OFFICER *strides off. Blackout. Silence.*

ACT TWO

Scene One

A hut on an airfield. A group of RAF *personnel, sitting, standing, talking, reading. An* AIRMAN *enters, followed by* BELA *in a dark overcoat. It is 1943.*

Drawing: GRIGOR'S *'Dead Woman after a Raid.'*

FIRST AIRMAN. Ladies and Gentlemen —
SECOND AIRMAN. Boys and girls —
FIRST AIRWOMAN. Comrades, surely?
FIRST AIRMAN. As you wish —
FIRST AIRWOMAN. What's wrong with comrades?
FIRST AIRMAN. Sorry to keep you waiting. We couldn't find the hut. The hut had vanished.
THIRD AIRMAN. It is always the same hut, Roger.
FIRST AIRMAN. Thank you, Don.
FIRST AIRWOMAN. Hut 48C.
FIRST AIRMAN. I'm indebted to you, Dorothy. *(He ushers* BELA *forward. Chairs shift, people sit.)* I would like most cordially, on behalf of the Brave New World Club, RAF Basingbourne, to welcome our most distinguished visitor, Mr Bela Veracek, better known to most of us as Vera of the *Daily Mirror* — er — *(He looks round.)* Where is the Distinguished Visitor's Chair, please? *(Everyone looks round.)* The DVC? *(He looks to* BELA.*)* Sorry about this. Has anyone seen the —
FIRST AIRWOMAN. Chopped it up.

Pause.

FIRST AIRMAN. Chopped it up?
FIRST AIRWOMAN. For firewood, yes.
FIRST AIRMAN. You did WHAT!
FIRST AIRWOMAN. Oh, come on, Roger —
THIRD AIRWOMAN. We had a bit of a discussion about it, and then we —
FIRST AIRWOMAN. Chopped it up.
BELA. It's perfectly all right, I'll sit down here —
FIRST AIRMAN. No, it's not that, it's —
FIRST AIRWOMAN *(to* BELA*)*. It's not that we don't want you to have a chair.
FIRST AIRMAN. Of course it's not —
FIRST AIRWOMAN. It's just that some of us — the hardliners in the struggle for cultural democracy — have always challenged the notion that distinguished visitors needed distinguished chairs —

FIRST AIRMAN.   That's all very well —
FIRST AIRWOMAN.   It burned very well, Roger. All the genius
  soaked in the wood. The sweaty palms of greatness. Went like paraffin.
  WOOF!

Pause.

FIRST AIRMAN.   Discuss this later.
THIRD AIRMAN.   Put it on the agenda, Michael!
FIRST AIRWOMAN.   Inquest on the DVC.
FIRST AIRMAN.   It isn't funny, Dorothy.
SECOND/THIRD AIRMEN *(shaking heads)*.   No — no — no —
FIRST AIRMAN.   We are self-governing, but we must have rules!
THIRD AIRMAN.   Yipee!
FIRST AIRMAN.   Rules, Don, yes —
SECOND AIRMAN.   Can't do nothink without yer rules —
FIRST AIRMAN.   That happens to be absolutely true, like it or not —
SECOND AIRWOMAN.   Look, we are being very bloody rude!

Pause.

FIRST AIRMAN.   Quite.
FIRST AIRWOMAN *(standing)*.   We welcome Vera. We feel very
  honoured. Could I offer you a rather ordinary chair?
BELA *(taking the chair from her)*.   Thank you, I am happy with any
  chair. *(He puts his hat on it.)* Beastly weather. *(He takes his coat off.)*
  No flying today. *(He folds his coat over the back of the chair, leans on it,
  clears his throat.)* I was born in Budapest on January 15th, 1898. I lived
  in Hungary until 1922. I lived in the Soviet Union until 1936. I am a
  cartoonist. I believe the cartoon to be the lowest form of art. I also
  believe it to be the most important form of art. I decided in my twenty-
  fourth year I would rather be important that great. I decided this
  because I have always preferred shouting to whispering and humanity
  more than myself. The cartoon is a weapon in the struggle of peoples.
  It is a liberating instrument. It is brief like life. It is not about me. It is
  about us. Important art is about us. Great art is about me. I am not
  interested in me. I do not like me. I am not sure if I like us either, but
  that is private and the cartoon is not private. We share the cartoon as
  we cannot share the painting. We plunder painting for the private
  meaning. The cartoon has only one meaning. When the cartoon lies it
  shows at once. When the painting lies it can deceive for centuries. The
  cartoon is celebrated in a million homes. The painting is worshipped in
  a gallery. The cartoon changes the world. The painting changes the
  artist. I long to change the world. I hate the world. Thank you.

Pause. He sits, blows his nose.

FIRST AIRMAN *(standing)*.   There we are, then. Plenty to chew on
  there. Mr Veracek has said he'll answer questions, so the meeting is
  open to the floor. First question, please. *(He sits.)* Or statement.
  Whatever you like. . . . *(Pause.)* I'm sure we're all bursting with

suggestions. *(Pause.)* Anyone? *(Pause.)* Margaret, I'm sure you —
(SECOND AIRWOMAN shakes her head curtly.) All right, I'll kick
off, then. *(He turns to BELA)* Mr Veracek, I've always wondered why
the papers are —
FOURTH AIRMAN. I DON'T LIKE THIS FUCKING WORLD
EITHER.

Pause.

FIRST AIRMAN. I don't think that's a question, Kenny, is it —
FOURTH AIRMAN. I DON'T LIKE IT ANY MORE THAN YOU.
SECOND AIRMAN. Got a question, put yer hand up —
FOURTH AIRMAN. QUESTION.
FIRST AIRMAN. I think I was asking something, wasn't I?
FOURTH AIRMAN *(standing)*. WHY ARE WE DROPPING PHOS-
PHOROUS BOMBS ON KIDS?
THIRD AIRMAN. Come on, Kenny —
FOURTH AIRMAN. I was doing Aachen last night, wasn't I?
FIRST AIRWOMAN. Sit down, Kenny —
FOURTH AIRMAN. ASKED A QUESTION!
SECOND AIRMAN. Always ask that question —
THIRD AIRMAN. Every bloody meeting, Kenny says —
FOURTH AIRMAN. BECAUSE I HAVEN'T GOT A FUCKING
ANSWER YET!
FIRST AIRWOMAN. We will hold a special meeting on the subject of
civilian bombing —
THIRD AIRMAN. Just for Kenny —
FIRST AIRWOMAN. Can we have that in the Suggestion Book?
FOURTH AIRMAN. DON'T WANT IT IN THE FUCKING
SUGGESTION BOOK! DON'T WANT YOU TO ANSWER IT!
WANT HIM TO ANSWER IT! *(Pause.)* Want genius to answer
it, see?

Pause.

BELA. This is a very good question.
FOURTH AIRMAN. Cheers. He says it's a good question.

He sits.

FIRST AIRWOMAN. It is not a good question. It is a confusing,
innaccurate question.
FOURTH AIRMAN. It's a question, ain't it?
FIRST AIRWOMAN. It is a stifling, suffocating question. It's a bog
question. I hate bog questions. I don't want to be sucked down in
Kenny's bog.
FOURTH AIRMAN. Well, answer it!
FIRST AIRWOMAN. Hitler has been gassing kids since 1938.
THIRD AIRMAN. 's not the answer, Dorothy. . . .
FIRST AIRMAN *(to BELA)*. Kenny is a tail-end gunner. Did his bit in
setting light to Rotterdam. . . .

FOURTH AIRMAN.   I'm sorry I can't draw. You do the cartoon for
    me.
FIRST AIRMAN.   I don't think we asked Mr Veracek here in order that
    he should —
SECOND AIRWOMAN.   Why not?
FIRST AIRWOMAN.   Kenny is trying to drag pacifist slogans into this
    discussion —
SECOND AIRMAN.   What discussion?
FIRST AIRWOMAN.   Correction. Kenny is trying to initiate a pacifist
    discussion —
SECOND AIRWOMAN.   He is asking for a practical demonstration of
    the cartoonist's art —
FIRST AIRWOMAN.   He is trying to annexe the meeting —
FIRST AIRMAN.   Can we get a bit of order here? We obviously can't
    ask Mr Veracek to take a pencil and just go —
SECOND AIRWOMAN.   He has just said the cartoon is the people's
    art. We are people, aren't we?
FIRST AIRMAN.   This is worse than when we had Bertrand Russell —
THIRD AIRMAN.   Bertrand Russell couldn't draw —
FOURTH AIRMAN *(stands, tosses a pencil).*   Here —
FIRST AIRWOMAN.   All right, if the cartoon represents the people
    it'll have to represent me too. It will have to include my view, which is
    the opposite of Kenny's. If they took female aircrew I would drop
    phosphorous.
THIRD AIRMAN.   On children?
FIRST AIRWOMAN.   Yes.
BELA.   I do not actually see how in a single cartoon I can reconcile such
    contrasting points of view. I do not see how in one drawing I can show
    both pacifism and support the war. I can only say I have to draw what
    speaks to me —
SECOND AIRWOMAN.   No. *(She stands.)* No. You see, you are
    talking about private art again. You are talking about painting. What
    you think. What strikes you. Artist stuff. Somewhere in the contra-
    dictions, there is the proper point of view. There is a correct one.
FIRST AIRWOMAN.   Absolutely.
SECOND AIRWOMAN.   It's a matter of finding it.

Pause. BELA *gets up, picks up his coat.*

FIRST AIRWOMAN.   Don't go!
BELA.   I have to, because you see —
FIRST AIRWOMAN.   NO, DON'T.

Pause.

BELA.   What you are saying I know will drive me mad!

Pause, then he turns to leave.

FIRST AIRMAN.   I'd like to thank Mr Veracek on behalf of every-
    one —

FOURTH AIRMAN. I COULD BE KILLED TONIGHT. *(BELA stops.)* Don't want it to be for nothing, see? *(BELA shakes his head, closing his eyes.)* Must have a little bit of truth to go with, please. . . .

SECOND AIRWOMAN. Draw the real war. Not Hitler. Easy hating Hitler. Too easy for a man like you. Draw the real war, will you? The war which goes on underneath the war? The long war of the English people. Draw that, please. . . .

BELA hesitates, then turns back, tossing down his hat. The room is full of cheering. Fade lights and silence. The airforce people leave. Sound of slamming doors and echoing footsteps on corridors. BELA does not move.

Scene Two

STRINGER, *an editor, comes in, looks at* BELA, *shakes his head.*

Sketch: BELA'S *cartoon 'There always was a Second Front'. An English Soldier is struggling with Hitler. A profiteer is trying to strangle the soldier from behind.*

STRINGER. I will do the talking, all right? Me. *(He crosses the room.)* You — you look small and intellectual. You look insignificant. Be a sort of bewildered academic rat. Got any spectacles? *(BELA takes out a pair, puts them on.)* No. Terrible. Smelly Bolshevik. *(He takes them off again.)* If they speak to you at all, what you say is things like this. 'This is a country I've admired all my life.' Okay? 'The King is a gentleman.' All right? 'Parliament is a national asset.' NOTHING CRITICAL AND DO NOT DEFEND YOURSELF. You have done wrong, all right? I want a sort of atmosphere of shame. I want this room to feel tacky with humility, I want tangible regret. I ask you to do this, Bela, because they do not like me and they want to shut the paper down. They have this act, this thing called the Defence of the Realm Act and it means they can shut papers down and stick the editors in gaol, all right? It's very like what Hitler's got. Only they had it long before Hitler. And it means we can end up in a concentration camp. And they had that long before Hitler, too. I don't want to end up on a draughty Scotish island nibbling sheep shit off the barbed wire, see? Highland cack for breakfast and galloping TB? No thank you. I don't want that and nor do you.

BELA. Nope.

STRINGER. Good. So be small. Be error incarnate.

There are voices off, loud and braying. STRINGER *prepares himself for his ordeal.* STRUBENZEE *enters. With two officials.*

STRUBENZEE. Good morning!

STRINGER *(offering his hand).* Sir Herbert —
STRUBENZEE. Hello, Bob — this is — Frank Deeds —
STRINGER. How d'ye do?
STRUBENZEE. And John Lowry —
STRINGER. Good morning —
STRUBENZEE. Hello, Bela!
LOWRY/DEEDS. Good morning.
STRUBENZEE. Bela Veracek.
LOWRY *(sitting at the desk).* Sit down, will you?
STRINGER. Here, okay?
LOWRY. Thank you. *(He clicks open his case.)* And you, Mr
    Veracek.*(*BELA *sits.* STRUBENZEE *looks out the window.)* cik, is
    it? Or cek?
STRINGER. Cek.
LOWRY *(ignoring* STRINGER*).* Cik is it, or cek?
BELA. Cek.
LOWRY. Thank you.
DEEDS. Look, don't want to lose the entire morning over this, so get to
    the point swiftly, shall we? Winston doesn't like this.
STRINGER. Ah.
DEEDS. He doesn't at all. In fact he hates it. And I don't like it either.
STRINGER. I see.
DEEDS. It's you-know-what, isn't it? Pure you-know-what.
STRINGER. I suppose it is.
DEEDS. Very much so. And we feel we want to crack down on it, don't
    we, John? Crack down on it very hard.
LOWRY. Anybody smoke, do they?

He vaguely offers a packet. No one accepts.

DEEDS. We agree about that, don't we?
LOWRY. Absolutely.
STRINGER. Yes, of course.
DEEDS. Coming back to Winston, I can assure you first thing this
    morning he was practically pissing blood. That's no exaggeration, is it,
    John?
LOWRY. No.
DEEDS. He was that cross.
STRINGER. I see.
LOWRY. Did the papers in bed, as usual.
DEEDS. As he always does, picks up the first one and there's this —
    this drawing, by this gentleman — and really, I can see his point. It is
    crude and ugly and utterly you-know-what.
STRINGER. Agreed.
DEEDS. Go on, John, will you?
LOWRY. He wants to shut your shop. . . .
STRINGER. Ah.
LOWRY. That was his first reaction. Shut the shop.
STRINGER. Ah.

DEEDS.   What do you say, Mr Veracek?

BELA *(with a shrug)*.   King George is a gentleman.

DEEDS.   Sorry?

BELA.   I am very fond of King George.

STRINGER.   I think you know the *Mirror* has backed Winston solidly since Munich.

LOWRY.   Yup.

STRINGER.   Uncritically.

LOWRY.   Yup.

STRINGER.   Has not wavered in its backing for the war effort.

LOWRY.   Yes.

STRINGER.   Supported every change in military command.

LOWRY.   Yes.

STRINGER.   Has been a wholly loyal and patriotic paper.

LOWRY.   Yes, and Winston recognizes this. Doesn't he, Frank? In his better moments recognizes it.

DEEDS.   Winston is thoroughly cognisant about the press. But feels you have abused his trust.

STRINGER.   I don't think so.

DEEDS.   Well, I say you have. And I am minded to close you down. What do you say, Mr Veracek?

BELA.   Parliament is the highest stage of human consciousness —

LOWRY.   I don't think Mr Veracek is being wholly —

STRINGER.   Bela is rather bewildered by all this —

DEEDS.   Is he so! Is he bewildered! Well, indeed! Perhaps you would inform him I am an officer of the King, that I have his warrant in my pocket here! King George VI of England, with all his many and diverse dominions, I am his voice, all right?

Pause.

STRINGER.   Yes.

DEEDS.   Good. I don't know about you, John, but I am minded to shut them down.

He leans back in his chair.

LOWRY.   You see, even if we were persuaded by you, and at this moment I must tell you I am not, we have an uphill struggle on our hands, a momentous task before us. We shall have to go from this room to Chequers and we shall get a rather rough ride, shan't we?

DEEDS.   Very rough.

LOWRY.   And I'm not prepared to do that if I don't feel wholly and completely satisfied. And I'm not.

Pause.

STRINGER.   You can't shut all the papers down.

DEEDS.   Oh, I can, I can! I have the warrant, yes I can!

STRINGER.   All right, you can —

DEEDS.   Oh, I can, Bob.

STRINGER. All the banned papers are small papers. The *Mirror* has one and a half million.

LOWRY. Slightly more, I think.

STRINGER. All right, yes. A growing circulation, and you can't just —

DEEDS. Do not keep telling me what I can and cannot do —

STRINGER. All right, I'm sorry, you have the power, obviously, but does it look good?

DEEDS. Well, I'm not sure we're all that bothered what it looks like, are we, John? Winston isn't.

STRINGER. Well, I'll put it another way —

DEEDS. Is anybody bringing tea? *(He looks round at STRUBENZEE.)* I did ask for tea, didn't I? I find it very peculiar to have to ask for it, but I did ask for it, all the same —

STRUBENZEE *(going to the door.)* I'll look —

DEEDS. Thank you — No, I'm perfectly clear-minded on the —

STRINGER. I was saying —

DEEDS. Sorry —

LOWRY. He was saying —

STRINGER. This is supposed to be a war for democracy. At least I believe that is the common comprehension of the people, and an expression of democracy, as I understand it, is a plurality of political opinion within the —

DEEDS. Quite.

Pause.

LOWRY. Within, you see.

DEEDS. Within.

STRINGER. Yes. Within an accepted frame of reference.

LOWRY. That's it. I don't think Mr Veracek, for all his love of parliament, is quite within. Are you, Mr Veracek? Within? *(BELA shrugs, looks at STRINGER.)* I mean, what are your politics, Mr Veracek?

STRINGER. I think that's Mr Veracek's own —

DEEDS. What are your politics?

LOWRY. I think his politics are you-know-what, aren't they? Going by the cartoon?

BELA. My politics are to look for the truth, and when you find it, shout it. That's my politics.

LOWRY. Very good. But what are your politics?

DEEDS. I don't want to bring up the point about Mr Veracek being an alien — not specifically at this point — but — well, I seem to have brought it up, don't I?

LOWRY. You have, I think —

DEEDS. Yes, I have brought it up now, so I may as well go on with it —

LOWRY. Yes —

DEEDS. Mr Veracek, you are only too aware, I'm sure, that you enjoy the status of an alien as far as King George and the Government's concerned, and what is more, an alien originating from a country with whom King George and the Government regard themselves as in a state of war, the so-called Magyar Republic — do you want to come in here, Herbert?

STRUBENZEE. Tea's on its way, I can see the trolley. . . .

DEEDS. Do you?

STRUBENZEE *(returning)*. Yes, you see Bela, we are under no very special obligations to you, coming here as you did from the territory of a country with whom we are at war —

BELA. The Soviet Union? We are not at war with the Soviet Union!

LOWRY. We are. *(He looks to the others.)* We are.

STRUBENZEE. It's a tricky one —

BELA. Someone should tell the English people! They are under the impression they are at war with Hitler!

STRUBENZEE. Well, so they are —

BELA. They are under the cruel misapprehension that it is Nazi bombers that are blowing their limbs off and killing children in their beds! How has this wicked deception been permitted?

STRINGER. Bela —

BELA. How is it Herr Hitler has been so cruelly discredited?

STRUBENZEE. The point is this —

LOWRY. Don't let him make a fool of you, Herbert, please.

STRUBENZEE. No — the point is this — that in a sense we are at war with the USSR, even though we are on the same side —

LOWRY. Dear, oh, dear —

STRUBENZEE. Under the Aliens Act, the authorities have special powers to place you in detention if it is deemed you represent a threat to national security —

LOWRY. Thank you.

DEEDS. And God knows, we may well deem it. Where is the tea?

BELA *(to STRINGER)*. I am being threatened with imprisonment.

STRUBENZEE. That is a very —

BELA. I AM BEING THREATENED WITH GAOL!

STRUBENZEE. No — no — not at all.

BELA. WHY ARE YOU TELLING ME THIS, THEN?

STRINGER. Bela, why don't you sit down?

BELA. WHY IS HE TELLING ME?

DEEDS *(as if a catechism)*. Tempra — mental — central — Euro — pean — intell — ectual — bore. . . .

LOWRY. The Home Office — its so colourful. . . .

STRUBENZEE. You are not helping, Frank —

BELA. I ask you why this conversation was begun!

STRUBENZEE. It was begun because Frank asked me to explain the provisions of the special powers act —

STRINGER. Bela, I will tell you what they're saying shall I? They are saying there is a very draughty, damp and disease-infected place where they stick foreign communists, all right? *(He looks at DEEDS.)* Now shut the paper down! We'll go out with a dirty great red-edged edition, banner headline seven inches high!

LOWRY.   Now, Bob, that's silly, isn't it?
DEEDS.   Bob's blown.
LOWRY.   It is particularly silly because of course we won't allow it —
DEEDS.   Never —
LOWRY.   We will shut you down from six o'clock tonight.
DEEDS.   Or now.
LOWRY.   Or now, even.
DEEDS.   I only have to pin this notice to the doors, and you can send the printers home.
LOWRY.   All right?
DEEDS.   This is a mighty piece of paper, Bob. *(He waves it.)* This paper says troops with bayonets on all the doors and lock the printers out. Now, where were we? Here's the tea.

A WOMAN enters with a trolley. She pours a number of cups in a strange silence, then turns to go.

BELA.   What do you think?
WOMAN *(stops)*.   Wha'? Me?
BELA.   WHAT DO YOU THINK OF THIS!
LOWRY.   Herbert —

He sips.

BELA.   THIS IS YOUR COUNTRY! LOOK WHAT THEY DO BEHIND CLOSED DOORS!
WOMAN.   Er —
STRUBENZEE.   Thank you. Just go.
BELA.   You're a human being, aren't you? Shout out won't stick this.
DEEDS.   Just go out, please.
BELA.   Don't just push the trolley, darling, fight!

She goes out. Pause.

DEEDS.   That is —
STRINGER.   I'm very sorry —
DEEDS.   No, listen, that is ABSOLUTELY NOT DONE HERE.
STRINGER.   I'm very sorry —
DEEDS.   IT MAKES ME ABSOLUTELY CERTAIN THAT I WANT TO SHUT YOU DOWN!
STRINGER.   I can see that —
STRUBENZEE.   Sugar, John?
DEEDS.   CERTAIN OF IT.
LOWRY.   All right, Frank. . . .

Pause. They drink. STRINGER beckons to BELA, takes him aside, to the window.

STRUBENZEE.   Biscuit?
DEEDS.   Drink the tea and close him.
LOWRY.   Have the tea first.
STRUBENZEE.   Biscuit?

STRINGER. Look out of the window, look at the street. What do you see?

BELA. People, of course!

STRINGER. Good. And in those people, somewhere, is the ONE WHO THINKS. Who, by miracle, or accident, or because his brain is kinked WILL SEE THROUGH THE FLANNEL. Who, by blinking at a lucky moment, sees through the great pouring curtain of piss. Let's not desert him. eh? Let's do our tiny little bit. *(Pause. BELA looks at him, shakes his head in weary resignation. STRINGER goes back to the others).* I beg pardon for the divisive cartoon. On bended knee I acknowledge the error of sowing seeds of dissension in the British people, of undermining the national effort and breeding an atmosphere of doubt. I will publish a rebuke of Vera in the first edition. I will vet all future submissions by this artist. I will arrange regular meetings at which we can discuss the paper's line. *(Pause.)* Can I carry on, or not?

Pause.

LOWRY. I think Bob's offer goes a long way towards —

DEEDS. I am very upset.

STRINGER. Yes.

DEEDS. I am very upset. You understand that, Bob?

LOWRY. Yes, we know you are, but this is virtually what we wanted, isn't it? This way we retain a plurality of papers. I could go to Chequers with an offer of that sort.

STRUBENZEE. It's voluntary, that's what's good about it, surely? Why use compulsion when people are toppling over backwards?

DEEDS. Bert, you have your department, I have mine.

STRUBENZEE. Yes.

DEEDS gets up, walks around.

DEEDS. Say it again.

STRINGER. Well, I can't remember the exact phrasing —

LOWRY. Apologize. Rebuke. And vet.

STRINGER. Yes.

Pause.

DEEDS. All right. Did I bring a coat?

LOWRY. Downstairs in the lobby.

STRINGER. Thank you.

LOWRY. Good-bye.

STRINGER. Thank you. Good-bye.

DEEDS. Cheerio, Bob.

He picks up his bag.

LOWRY *(to BELA).* Cheerio.

They depart. Pause.

STRUBENZEE.   Anybody want a drink?
STRINGER.   Urgently.
STRUBENZEE.   Good. Bela?

BELA *shakes his head.*

STRINGER.   Why not?

BELA *shakes his head again.*

STUBENZEE.   Oh, come on!
STRINGER.   No. . . .

They go out. BELA *stands there. The* WOMAN *comes back for the tea.*

WOMAN.   Left you, have they? On your own - ee - o? Never mind.

She puts the teacups on the trolley.

BELA.   Supposing freedom's not the truth? Have you ever thought of
   that? Suppose the truth's somewhere else after all? *(She looks at him.)*
   I go about, I shove the thermometer of freedom in the great wet gob of
   humanity and I go, good, we're healthy, when the mercury goes up,
   and bad, we're ill, when the mercury goes down. The fever of truth.
   Suppose freedom's nothing to do with it? Suppose it's just a virus?
   Suppose the truth is love?
WOMAN.   You never know.
BELA.   You don't. *(She goes to move away.)* I mean, you've only got
   one life, haven't you?
WOMAN.   That's for sure.
BELA.   Got to use it properly. haven't you? No good being on your
   deathbed and saying, fuck, I got it wrong, I was up the wrong tree.
   That would be silly.
WOMAN.   Bloody silly.
BELA.   Got to use it, haven't you? Use it all up, like toothpaste, to the
   bottom of the tube, Squeeze! Squeeze!
WOMAN.   That's it!

She starts to go again.

BELA.   Are you using yours up?
WOMAN.   Good question.

Pause.

BELA.   Got children, have you? Got a man somewhere?
WOMAN.   Two kids in Clapham. Old man in the infantry.
BELA.   Give us a kiss.

Pause.

WOMAN.   Better not.
BELA.   Better not, she says. Why better not? What's better about it?
WOMAN.   You know what kissing leads to.
BELA.   No . . . where does it lead? *(Pause. She goes to move off.)* I
   used to draw women.

WOMAN.   Oh?
BELA.   Drawn lots of women in my time. You have a lovely back.
WOMAN.   Do I?
BELA.   It's very strong and beautiful, your back.

*She doesn't move, but stands still, looking away from him. He runs his
hands across her shoulder. Pause. He turns away again.*

WOMAN.   What's the matter?
BELA.   I'm sorry. I'm not a good man.
WOMAN.   I don't mind that.
BELA.   Talk drivel just to get you — just to — lies and stuff —
WOMAN.   Don't matter. Got to, haven't you? Got to go through that.
   For what we want. Never mind that. (*She turns, looks at him.*) No
   more going down the underground.
BELA.   Can't keep the bombs off. With my little drop of love.
WOMAN.   No? Why not?

Fade to black.

Scene Three

*A solitary figure is sweeping a path in a London Park. He has a systematic
movement, eyes on the ground.* BELA *appears. Watches him. It is 1960.*

Drawing: GRIGOR's *last drawing. A horribly emaciated female figure in
a posture of rejection. As the last phase of* GRIGOR's *nude drawing it is
violently distorted and pained.*

BELA.   Did you do much queuing, friend? (GRIGOR *ignores him.*)
   Your feet look like feet that have shuffled down endless corridors. . . .
   (*Pause.*) And your head is like a head bowed down by the drizzle of
   futile interviews. . . . (*Pause.*) And the way you hold that broom, like
   it's a rock and you'd be swept away if someone took it from you. (*He
   goes towards him.*) Grigor, I shan't take your broom away —
   (Suddenly GRIGOR *lifts the dustbin out of the little cart, raises it above
   his head and flings it down. Beer cans roll across the stage. Pause.*) Glad
   to see me, I can tell.

Pause.

GRIGOR.   Council given me a flat, okay!
BELA.   That's good.
GRIGOR.   Given me overalls, okay!
BELA.   Very smart —
GRIGOR.   SIX POUND A WEEK!
BELA.   Yes —

GRIGOR.   OKAY!

He stares at the ground. Pause.

BELA.   Buy paint with that?
GRIGOR.   Buy paint.
BELA.   Oils?
GRIGOR.   Oils.
BELA.   Good.
GRIGOR.   By numbers.
BELA.   What?
GRIGOR.   By numbers!

Pause.

BELA.   Paint by numbers?
GRIGOR.   Done good. Done flower garden. Difficult. Done Good
   Queen Bess. Difficult, oh, fucking difficult.
BELA.   Go on.
GRIGOR.   Done cat. Done dog.
BELA.   Lecture me, Grigor. Lecture me on the point of art.
GRIGOR.   Done Windsor Castle.
BELA.   On the function of a line. What the line does, Grigor. Line does
   not exist in nature. Line is an invention of mankind. Go on, Grigor. . . .
   (Pause. GRIGOR doesn't move.) Line is the means by which we venture
   in to the formlessness of nature, which guides us through the labyrinth.
   (GRIGOR is motionless.) He who draws a line puts form on
   formlessness. The line describes unconsciousness. Draw me a little
   picture, Grigor. Draw me a picture of your mind. . . .

Pause.

GRIGOR.   Done Yankee Windjammer. Oh, fucking difficult! Tricky
   little sails — and —
BELA.   What happened in the wood, Grigor?
GRIGOR.   Rigging — difficult.
BELA.   WHAT HAPPENED IN THE WOOD! *(Pause. GRIGOR
   doesn't react. After a few moments, he begins picking up the beer cans,
   tossing them in the bin. BELA watches, then joins him, kneeling on the
   ground, filling up his arms. Suddenly he stops.)* Got to keep sane! Got to
   keep my lovely head! Last decent brain in Europe! Oh, mind my head!
   Don't cross the road! Look out for bricks and bottles falling off of flats!
   Got the truth there! Oh, look after it! *(He drops the cans, staggers to his
   feet, his arms wrapped round his head to protect it.)* Mind out! My
   precious head! My head!

*He careers offstage, clasping his head awkwardly. Blackout. Sound of lift
rising, doors opening.*

Scene Four

The office of the manager of a daily paper. He sits in a Swedish chair. Lights up on his extended hand. A figure enters in a suit.

Sketch: BELA'S *'They Grew Tired of Thought'. A spectacular panorama of Europe in a nuclear fire. Heaped with corpses, and above it a monstrous deformity in mask and goggles.*

MIK *(shaking* DIVER'S *hand).* I brought my folder. For your delectation.
DIVER. Do you drink?
MIK. All day long.
DIVER. For inspiration?
MIK. No. Intoxication. Shall I sit?
DIVER *(reaching for a bottle).* We love your work.
MIK. Thank you. I'm rather fond of it myself.

Pause. Diver's hand remains on the bottle.

DIVER. Can I just say, before we go any further, you need not feel under any obligation to be witty talking to me. Of course we know you're funny, that's why you're here, so you don't have to prove anything, all right?
MIK. Sorry.
DIVER. If you talk like that all the time, all well and good, but don't put yourself out, okay?
MIK. Sorry. Nerves.
DIVER. Of course. Whisky?
MIK. Thank you.

Pause, while DIVER *squirts the syphon.*

DIVER. We have a very fine cartoonist on this paper.
MIK. Vera.
DIVER. Vera, yes. I say a cartoonist, but he's more than a cartoonist. He's a visionary.
MIK. Absolutely.
DIVER. He is a genius. But Lord Slater feels — correctly if you take that point of view — that there is not a lot of comedy there. Lord Slater says he hasn't actually laughed at Vera now for fifteen years.
MIK. He's not a barrel of laughs.
DIVER. That is exactly what Lord Slater said. He is not a barrel of laughs. As you know, Lord Slater has owned nearly every paper in the world at some time or the other, excluding *Pravda* and the Peking *People's Daily,* and he has come to the conclusion, in his wisdom, that human beings need to laugh.
MIK. Absolutely.
DIVER. You agree with Lord Slater then?
MIK. I do.
DIVER. Good. Because this is where you come in. Lord Slater isn't

looking for a genius.

MIK. No problem.

DIVER. No problem with you, no.

MIK. No one's ever called me a genius.

DIVER. Nor likely to?

MIK. I shouldn't think so.

DIVER. Have another drink.

MIK. Thank you.

DIVER *refills.*

DIVER. Lord Slater's sense of humour — and he admits this — is altogether basic. He can actually laugh — I do mean laugh —

MIK. Ha, ha —

DIVER. Quite — actually laugh at postcards which show bald Englishmen at the seaside who have lost their dicks — *(*MIK *laughs loudly.)* Can choke himself at pictures of fat women who are manifestly sexually deprived — *(*MIK *laughs loudly again.)* He finds that genuinely funny.

MIK *(shaking his head.)* Terrific. . . .

DIVER. Well, I think you're just the man he's looking for. What shall I call you? Do you like to be called Mik?

MIK. Suits me.

DIVER. Yes, I think it does.

MIK. My real name's Michael, but at art school I cut it down to Mik.

DIVER. You have been trained, have you?

MIK. Doesn't it show?

DIVER. I'm no expert, Mr Mik. Just one other thing. As well as being terribly funny, Lord Slater is very keen for you to have a point of view. Do you have a point of view?

MIK. I think life's a non-stop comedy show.

DIVER. Yes, quite, but I think Lord Slater was thinking more along the lines of — well, to take his own example, do you like trade unions?

MIK. Well, to be quite —

DIVER. Lord Slater doesn't madly, you see.

MIK. Me neither.

DIVER. There we are, then. Would you like to see yourself out?

MIK *(draining his drink).* Thank you very much for seeing me. *(He picks up his folder, starts to go.)* Is Vera going, then?

DIVER. Vera is 75. *(*MIK *goes out.* DIVER *walks a little way round the room,* BELA *comes in, arms entwined about his head. He sits without ceremony in* DIVER's *chair.)* Ah, Bela —

BELA. Oh, this is a dirty place. Have to wear my old coat here, see? Got my old mac on. Great dirty place this Fleet Street. How do you stick it? Don't your wife say when you come in, don't bring that muck in here! Better be a coalminer, it comes off with a bit of soap, but you, in bed with your soft white Mrs, carry in the sheets your little smears. . . .

DIVER. We always have to go through this. . . .

BELA. That's why you change your secretary every week. Never got the same one has he? Think you lose your dirt by going through all this knicker, but you don't, if anything gets worse. Try to block your nostrils with girl smells and the Johnny Walker! No, Anthony, this stink comes from inside, rotting brain. . . .

DIVER. Thank you, Bela. . . .

BELA. No, don't thank me, I say this because I look at you and I have to say, is this a way to live?

DIVER *(looking at BELA's absurd posture)*. Ah. . . .

BELA. Now you think I envy you, you think I'm spiteful because I'm old, you think I want to suck your secretary, no, I don't, believe me I don't, I only say go and stand in a bit of daylight, there ain't no daylight here, look at these lights, you live in soft mad places, don't you, all girls and carpets, see yourself for what you are, another man's thing, you got no freedom, only Johnny Walker.

DIVER. Thank you.

BELA. That's all right, I want to help. It's what they used to give the natives, see? Liquor and cunt? You a native, are you?

DIVER. I suppose I am.

BELA. Poor old English native. *(He pretends to call someone.)* 'ere, give the man another crate!

DIVER. How are you, Bela? How's your head?

BELA. It's okay as long as I take care of it. I don't know why I come here, though, I don't like towns, so fucking dangerous, all scaffolding and them great cranes, I don't like nothing above my head but sky. Only safe place, Salisbury Plain.

DIVER. I'm very grateful to you, coming up like this.

BELA. Of course that ain't safe either. There's no safe place, there never was one. Look at that ceiling, smooth, ain't it, looks fine, looks perfect, but underneath the plaster, how many little parasites? Them great steel joists, how much metal strain? You go down the escalator, lovely shiny tiles and all them clean girls with the tits and bras, but just behind it, mud and clay, pressing, pressing to get in, wanting to burst through and stuff your mouth with earth.

DIVER. You can never be sure —

BELA. Always, you make something, and from that moment, from that second, everything works to its destruction, everything racing to decay. I talk so much because I haven't seen no one for five days. What did you ask me here for?

DIVER. I think absolutely everything you say is absolutely true.

BELA. It is true, 'course it's true, but it's a truth you can't do nothing about. When you're old you think of all the things that can't be done, and when you're young you think of all the things that can. The young are best. Give us a fact you can grasp in your fingers, and all the rest, in the bin with it. I am a materialist. I always was a materialist, God bless it. There, I contradict myself, but then I always have. What am I here for, Anthony?

DIVER. Well, to talk.

BELA. Obviously.

DIVER. So I can sip a little at the well of wisdom. My little sparrow brain. My little hungry beak.

BELA. That's good. . . .

DIVER. Goes dip, dip, dip. . . .

BELA. Dip, dip, dip. . . .

DIVER. Bela, I've got the job of murdering you. *(Pause.)* My seedy little business. My calm and dirty duty. *(Pause.)* Going home to bed, as you say, caked. *(Pause.)* The black bits in between my toes —

BELA. NEVER MIND MY FUCKING METAPHORS.

Pause.

DIVER. Yes. *(Pause.)* I wonder if you'll hear me out? *(Pause.)* You see, the feeling exists —

BELA. THE FEELING EXISTS!

DIVER. No, I didn't think you would —

BELA. THE FEELING EXISTS!

DIVER. Yes —

BELA. NO SUCH FUCKING THING. Feelings don't exist. What do you think they are? Floating around in the air? Pluck 'em do you, whizzing past like wasps? Who feels the feeling, Anthony?

DIVER. Well, all right —

BELA. If it stinks, if it rots your little conscience, in the passive tense it goes! Nuclear devices were dropped — shots were fired — feelings exist — No! Say it in your person, I DROPPED, I FIRED, I FEEL!

DIVER. Very well —

BELA. I was a poet, but I got to hate words, do you see why? There is a great wide river flowing out the bottom of this building, a river of words, newsprint pouring over the waterfalls of inking machines and streaming through the city, washing men away with lies, the great flood of dirtiness, hold your heads up in the swell! Where is the ark? I AM. I AM NOAH, GET ON BOARD!

DIVER. Very good, very like one of your drawings, but this is precisely
.   where the board —

BELA. Why don't you say it?

DIVER. Say it? Say what?

BELA. YOU HATE ME.

DIVER *(bewildered).* Hate —

BELA. Hate me because I see! Like a great snake of blindmen tapping sticks, heading for the cliff edge, HATE THE MAN WHO SEES. I SEE. I GOT THE VISION AND YOU HATE ME!

DIVER. Bela!

BELA. You do! You do!

DIVER. Will you let me —

BELA. Rather fall off than hear the MAN WHO SEES!

DIVER. Let me finish, will you please?

BELA. Finish? Finish what?

DIVER. I PREPARED THIS FUCKING SPEECH. *(Pause. BELA*

shrugs contemptuously.) Because it hurts me, too. You aren't the only one with pain. You aren't the only well of suffering. Dip my bucket just as deep. . . .

BELA.   You call that pain? That's not pain. Just a little leak of guilt. Just a damp patch on your Y-Fronts. . . .

Pause.

DIVER.   You are so arrogant. So terribly arrogant. *(Pause.)* It is the board's feeling that there is a quality of — depression — in your work — of nihilism — which makes it inappropriate — I summarize, of course, to a national, family newspaper. *(Pause.)* And anyway, you're 75.

He goes to pick up the whisky bottle and pour a drink. BELA knocks it flying.

BELA.   Liquor don't give me the sack!
DIVER. *(seeing the liquid on his suit).*   You're going a little bit —
BELA.   Not Johnny fucking Walker kicking Bela Veracek downstairs! You do it. Don't get Johnny in.

Pause. DIVER wipes his fingers on a handkerchief.

DIVER.   The Corporation want to publish a collection of your work. . . . In hard and paperback.
BELA.   Never.
DIVER.   Bela —
BELA.   Never! I ain't for putting on girl's laps and kissing over. I ain't art!
DIVER.   Think about it —
BELA.   Anthony, don't you see? They want to make me into art, do you know why? 'cos art don't hurt. Look at Goya. His firing squad — I seen it on stockbroker's walls! But I still hurt, see? I touch their little pink nerve with my needle, like the frog's legs on the bench. I shock their muscle and they TWITCH! They don't want to twitch, see? They're so much happier lying dead! But I twitch 'em! I SHOCK THE BASTARDS INTO LIFE!

Pause.

DIVER.   Yes. . . . *(Pause.)* Yes. . . . *(He goes to the intercom.)* Jane! *(Pause.)* Bring in a cloth, will you?

Pause, then a SECRETARY enters, holding an old towel. DIVER indicates the spilt whisky. She kneels, rubs the carpet. They watch her.

BELA.   Oh, darling, all your sweet bits. . . .I've not touched you so much with all my genius as one groove of a loud boy's disc. . . .

Blackout.

Scene Five

The sound of Big Ben. It is a dark night in the pool of London. Two officers of the River Police are seen observing the figure of an old man silhouetted on the parapet of Tower Bridge. PC DOCKERILL *holds a loud hailer.*

DOCKERILL.   YOU ARE NOT ALLOWED TO JUMP IN THE WATER. CAN YOU HEAR ME? YOU ARE NOT ALLOWED TO JUMP IN THE WATER.
BELA. I wish to die.
DOCKERILL.   THIS RIVER IS FULL OF GERMS.
BELA.   I am not afraid of germs. I am a germ. You are a germ. The human race is a germ.
DOCKERILL.   WHO ARE YOU CALLING A GERM?
HOOGSTRATEN.   I'll do the talking, Michael.
DOCKERILL.   WHO'S 'E CALLING A FUCKIN' GERM?
HOOGSTRATEN.   Michael — *(He takes the Hailer.)* Good-evening. This is John here.
BELA.   John who.

Pause.

HOOGSTRATEN.   PC John. Metropolitan River Police.
BELA.   Look, John, get your boat away.
HOOGSTRATEN.   Why don't we talk this over eh?
BELA.   No.
HOOGSTRATEN.   You see, I don't think you want to die at all. You just want a bit of attention.
BELA.   Thank you, I have had all the attention I want.
HOOGSTRATEN.   Tell us about it.
BELA.   I don't want to discuss my life, I want to finish it! So kindly shift your motorboat.
HOOGSTRATEN.   Now listen — *(The hailer goes off.)* What's the matter with this — *(It comes on.)* Now listen. I've done a course in psychology —
BELA.   I HATE PSYCHOLOGY.
HOOGSTRATEN.   You what?
BELA.   I HATE PSYCHOLOGY! I HATE MAGIC!
HOOGSTRATEN.   All right, you don't like it —
BELA.   Why can't you just let a man —
DOCKERILL.   'COS IT'S AN OFFENCE, ALL RIGHT? THAT's WHY!
HOOGSTRATEN.   Michael —
DOCKERILL.   BIN UP ALL FUCKING NIGHT FISHING BUGGERS OUT THE WATER!
HOOGSTRATEN.   Michael —
DOCKERILL.   What is it about Saturdays?
HOOGSTRATEN.   You see — no one really wants to die.
BELA.   I do.

HOOGSTRATEN. No. You only think you do.
BELA. Of course I think I do.
HOOGSTRATEN. That's it, you see.
BELA. What is?
HOOGSTRATEN *(desperately)*. How old are you?
BELA. 75.
HOOGSTRATEN *(delight)*. 75! How about that? 75, Michael!
DOCKERILL. WHAT IS IT, YER GAS BILL?
HOOGSTRATEN. 75! A wonderful age!
DOCKERILL. LOOK, GO AN' LAY YER 'EAD ACROSS A
    RAILWAY TRACK, ALL RIGHT? JUST DON'T JUMP IN MY
    RIVER —
HOOGSTRATEN. Michael —
DOCKERILL. COS I AIN'T PULLIN' YER OUT.
BELA. Thank Christ for a good man.
HOOGSTRATEN. Michael, that is just about the —

BELA *jumps*.

BELA. Thank you, thank you!
HOOGSTRATEN. Fuck. Fuck.

The engine revs up. Blackout.

Scene Six

The grounds of a hospital. A group of male NURSES *are grouped round a
patient in a wheelchair. The patient is staring with intense concentration at a
bedpan some yards away on the grass.*

Sketch: BELA*'s 'They Grew Tired of Thought'.*

FIRST NURSE. Come on! Come on!
SECOND NURSE. Lift it! Lift it!
THIRD NURSE. Make it a fiver, Barry?
FIRST NURSE. Doing it! Doing it!
THIRD NURSE. Where?
FIRST NURSE. Doing it!
THIRD NURSE. Where?
FOURTH NURSE. MOVED! I SAW IT!
THIRD NURSE. Where?
SECOND NURSE. Lift it! Lift it!
FIRST NURSE *(pointing)*. WHASSAT!
THIRD NURSE. Fuckin' ain't, yer know —
FIRST NURSE. WHASSAT!
THIRD NURSE *(kneeling by the bedpan)*. Nothing. . . .

FIRST NURSE.   Bloody did — it sort of —
THIRD NURSE.   Nothing!
FIRST NURSE.   Shuddered —

The patient is showing signs of stress.

THIRD NURSE *(contemptuously)*.   Shuddered. . . .
SECOND NURSE.   Lift it!
FIRST NURSE.   It's gonna go! It's gonna go!
THIRD NURSE.   Gotta be off the ground, Roy. . . .
SECOND NURSE.   Come on! Come on!
THIRD NURSE.   See daylight underneath it. . . .
SECOND NURSE.   Come on!
THIRD NURSE.   No daylight no payout. . . .
FIRST/FOURTH.   MOVE IT! MOVE IT! MOVE IT!
THIRD NURSE.   Who's fuckin' doin' it? 'im or you?
SECOND NURSE.   's'going!

With a cry of despair the patient falls back in his chair.

FIRST NURSE.   'e did it! 'e did it!
THIRD NURSE.   Bollocks —
FIRST NURSE.   Did it!
THIRD NURSE.   Daylight, Roger. . . .
GRIGOR.   CAN'T CONCENTRATE! CAN'T CONCENTRATE!
FIRST NURSE.   It moved mate. . . .
THIRD NURSE.   I am not accepting cheques. . . .
FIRST NURSE *(taking out his wallet)*.   It moved, Don. . . .
GRIGOR.   Air got . . . too heavy, see?
THIRD NURSE *(taking money all round)*.   Thank you. . . .
GRIGOR.   Started to . . . air got heavy. . . .
THIRD NURSE.   I can change a fiver, Clive. . . .
GRIGOR.   First, the object's got to chuck off all its habits, see? Got to
   stop being a piss pan, see? Think of itself like something else.
THIRD NURSE.   Three pounds, change.
GRIGOR.   Got to be God's will —
SECOND NURSE.   That's it, mate —
THIRD NURSE.   Thank you —
GRIGOR *(seized as if from beyond)*.   DO IT AGAIN! COMING
AGAIN!
FOURTH NURSE.   'ello, 'ello!
GRIGOR *(rigid in his chair)*.   COMING AGAIN!
THIRD NURSE.   Gentlemen, lay your bets!
GRIGOR.   I feel His spirit over me! God's body floating over London!
   Hold tight, please!
FIRST NURSE.   Ding! Ding!
THIRD NURSE.   Two pound, Barry? Two pounds anyone?
SECOND NURSE.   Okay —
THIRD NURSE.   Two pounds!
GRIGOR.   I draw Him in! He comes! I am the vessel of His will!

THIRD NURSE.   Roger? A sheet?
GIRIGOR.   My ol' skin, my ol' bones, got God in 'em!
FOURTH NURSE.   Fifty pence.
THIRD NURSE.   Clive, living dangerously. . . .
GRIGOR.   READY, GOD!
THIRD NURSE.   Daylight! Daylight pays!
SECOND NURSE.   Shuddup!
FIRST NURSE.   Shh!

GRIGOR'S *face assumes maximum tension. They stare at the bedpan.*

GRIGOR.   Neck . . . Neck!

SECOND NURSE *hurries to massage his neck.*

FIRST NURSE.   Lift — Lift —

They stare. Suddenly FOURTH NURSE *drops to his knees.*

FOURTH NURSE.   Somethin'! Somethin'!

GRIGOR *groans.*

THIRD NURSE.   Daylight. . . .
FIRST NURSE.   'S COMIN!
THIRD NURSE.   Daylight only. . . .
FOURTH NURSE.   Yes! Yes!

THIRD NURSE *hurries over, kneels to look.*

THIRD NURSE.   What?
FOURTH NURSE.   Yes!
THIRD NURSE.   What? What?

GRIGOR *shudders violently, lets out a cry.*

SECOND/FIRST/FOURTH.   YE — ES!

They begin clapping. The bedpan has not moved.

THIRD NURSE.   What, fuck it, what!

Amidst this feverish applause, BELA *enters in a wheelchair, pushed by*
DOCTOR GLASSON.
GLASSON *(gazing, shaking her head.)* Oh, Jesus bloody Christ. . . .
    *(*GRIGOR *lets out a long wail, his head falls back. Sheepishly, the*
    NURSES *withdraw.)* Whatcha trying to do? Drive the ol' boy barmy?
GRIGOR.   God says —
GLASSON *(of the bedpan).*   That's for pissing in, not praying to.
GRIGOR.   God says —
GLASSON.   Shuddup, I'm taking yer temperature! *(She shoves a*
    thermometer in his mouth.) If I was going to drown myself, I'd do it up at
    Henley. It's cleaner. Yer don't get contraceptives stuck in yer throat. Or
    Clivden. All those lovely beech trees and conspiring aristocrats. Might
    catch a glimpse of you out the library windows. . . . People are so boring
    when they die. Tiny little deaths in rooms, not making a nuisance. Same

way as they were conceived, I suppose . . . quietly, on a sofa. . . . Come
and go without a trace. Why don't we scratch our little mark, I wonder?
Claw some little protest on the granite ball? *(She looks offstage.)* Look
at 'em, peering through the railings. . . . IT'S ALL RIGHT, WE'RE
ALL BARMY IN 'ERE! Schoolgirls bunking off lessons, . . . wait till
yer married and the old man beats yer up, the kids 'ave got the whooping
cough and the rent goes up — KEEP A BED WARM FOR YER! *(She
turns back to* GRIGOR. *She removes the thermometer.)* I declare you
normal. I declare you fit to proceed with your extraordinary life, with all
its richness colour, vigour, thrills. I'm getting a cup of tea. Don't run
away. *(She turns to* BELA*)* And don't talk!

She goes off. Pause.

GRIGOR.   Hern the Hunter has been seen at Windsor Castle. *(Pause.)*
Oi. *(Pause.)* Hern the Hunter. *(Pause.)* Fuckin' Hern, see? AIN'T
BEEN SEEN SINCE 1931. *(Pause.)* Oi. *(Pause.)* Two comets crossed
tails over Peking. You listening? *(Pause.)* Oi. Got a message for yer. Oi.
DONCHA WANNA MESSAGE? *(Pause.)* We don't live alone. All
right? Always these happenings, see? Spirit world like an overcoat.
Invisible overcoat. They tell us, you born naked. BOLLOCKS.
BALLS. You born in garments of OTHER SPHERES. Oi. *(Pause.)* Oi.
Ain't gotta be what you are, see? That's the message. *(Pause.)* WHAT'S
THE MATTER? YOU DEAF? Pisspan. Don't 'ave to be a pisspan,
see? *(He stares at the bedpan. Slowly, it rises off the floor, remains
suspended about ten feet up.)* Wants to be a bird, see? Wants to be a bird!

BELA *looks. Suddenly he lets out a scream.*

BELA.   HELP! HELP! *(The pan drops with a clatter.* FIRST *and*
SECOND NURSES *rush in.)* Get him away from me! Bloody madman,
get him off me!
GRIGOR.   I am Grigor Gabor, I got God with me!
BELA.   There ain't no God! There ain't no Grigor!
SECOND NURSE.   Shuddup, the pair of yer!
BELA.   Gotta fight him! Fight barminess!
GRIGOR.   Got Christ in my ol' body, peace, He says! Peace, He says!
SECOND NURSE.   Get him out, Roger —
BELA.   He hurts my earholes, get him out! He gives me pains here. *(He
touches his head.)* Gives me murder, get him out!

SECOND NURSE, *wheels* GRIGOR *away.* GLASSON *enters.*

GLASSON.   'e does speak!
BELA.   GET HIM AWAY FROM ME!
GLASSON.   All right, darling, he's gone.
BELA.   I knew him! I knew him! Always 'is fucking spirit! I don't want 'is
spirit! Gets me here!

GLASSON *takes his hand.*

GLASSON.   Come on sweetheart, give us yer hand, give us yer hand —

(BELA *is weeping. She cradles his head.* SECOND NURSE *watches, uncomfortable.*) The tears, the tears! This place is floating on tears! Slippery stairs and slippery ceilings, I go 'ome wet to my bra, like a nursing mother, soddened with the milk of old men's weeping! Straight to the bath I go, down the plug'ole with your misery. . . !

SECOND NURSE. Take 'im back, shall I?

GLASSON. No!

SECOND NURSE. Time for 'is — .

GLASSON. Barry, fuck off, please!

He goes out. Pause. GLASSON *wipes* BELA's *eyes, sits on the grass, draws up her knees, looks at him. Pause.*

BELA *(in disbelief).* The piss pan. . . . Pisspan went up in the air. . . .

GLASSON. Yup.

BELA. DID IT? *(She nods.)* Christ. . . .

GLASSON. 'e does. . . . I'm afraid 'e does. . . . (BELA *sobs again, bitterly.)* Shall I kill you? Because I can, you see. I do it all the time. The people who won't go on swallowing the castor oil of life. The daily dose of pain and gibberish. It's there, see? The lying, the barmy, the savage, all swimming in the spoon. If you can't swallow it, I'll do it. If we'urt your brain to much. . . .

Pause.

BELA. All gone mad. . . .

GLASSON. No. That isn't it.

BELA. GONE MAD.

GLASSON. That isn't it. Don't give into that. *(Pause.)* You build your little temple, somewhere in the bottom of your brain, put brass doors on it, and great big hinges, burn your little flame of truth and genius and worship it, WHAT ABOUT US? *(She points to the cartoon.)* THAT DON'T 'ELP US! *(Pause.)* Assign the blame. *(Pause.)* It's madness if yer don't. Cos that's how we go on, blame this, blame that, get it wrong sometimes, of course, but never say we're barmy, or we will be. . . . *(Pause.)* Tea's cold. . . .

She gets up, Pause.

BELA. Give us a pencil . . . somebody. . . . *(He staggers out of the chair, advances towards audience.)* Give us a pencil . . . give us a pencil . . . give us a pencil. . . .

Fade to black.

THE END

STOCK PLAYS FROM JOHN CALDER

The following plays and playscripts, some of which were formerly published by Calder and Boyars, are now distributed exclusively by John Calder (Publishers) Ltd.

Plays	Cloth	Paper
Arthur Adamov		
Paolo Paoli	£4.95 & £1.95	
John Antrobus		
You'll Come to Love Your Sperm Test (New Writers 4)	£4.95 & £2.25	
Fernando Arrabal		
Plays Vol. 1 (Orison, Fando and Lis, The Car Cemetery, The Two Executioners)	£4.95 & £2.95	
Plays Vol. 2. (Guernica, The Labyrinth, The Tricycle, Picnic on the Battlefield, The Condemned Man's Bicycle)	£4.95 & £2.25	
Plays Vol. 3. (The Architect and the Emperor of Assyria, The Grand Ceremonial, The Solemn Communion)	£4.50 & T.O.P.	
Samuel Beckett		
Come and Go	75p	
Stewart Conn		
The Burning	£2.25	
Copi		
Plays Vol. 1	£4.95 & £1.95	
Marguerite Duras		
Three Plays (Days in the Trees, The Square, The Viaducts of Seine-et-Oise)	£4.95 & T.O.P.	
The Rivers and the Forests (*contained in* The Afternoon of M. Andesmas)	£4.95	
Suzanna Andler (*also* La Musica *and* L'Amante Anglaise)	£6.95 & £2.95	
Eugene Ionesco		
Three Plays (The Killer, The Chairs, Maid to Marry)	£2.25	
Plays Vol. 1. (The Chairs, The Bald Prima Donna, The Lesson, Jacques)	£5.95 & £2.95	
Plays Vol. 2. (Amédée, The New Tenant, Victims of Duty)	£4.95 & £2.95	
Plays Vol. 3. (The Killer, Improvisation, Maid to Marry)	£4.95 & £2.25	
Plays Vol. 4 (Rhinoceros, The Leader, The Future is in Eggs)	£4.95 & £2.95	
Plays Vol. 5. (Exit the King, The Motor Show, Foursome)	£4.95 & T.O.P.	
Plays Vol. 6. (A Stroll in the Air, Frenzy for Two)	£4.95 & £2.25	
Plays Vol. 7. (Hunger and Thirst, The Picture, Anger, Salutation)	T.O.P. & T.O.P.	
Plays Vol. 8. (Here Comes a Chopper, The Oversight, The Foot of the Wall)	£4.95 & T.O.P.	
Plays Vol. 9. (Macbett, The Mire, Learning to Walk)	£4.95 & T.O.P.	
Plays Vol. 10 (Oh, What a Bloody Circus, The Hardboiled Egg, *and* Ionesco and His Early English Critics)	£5.95 & £2.95	
Plays Vol. 11. (The Man with the Luggage, The Duel, Double Act, Why Do I Write?)	£5.95 & £2.95	
Robert McLellan		
Collected Plays Vol. 1. (Torwatletie, Jamie the Saxt, The Flowers o Edinburgh, The Carlin Moth *and* The Changeling)	£6.95	
Jamie the Saxt	£5.95 & £2.50	
David Mercer		
Belcher's Luck	£4.95 & T.O.P.	
Collected TV Plays Vol. 1. (Where the Difference Begins A Climate of Fear, The Birth of a Private Man)	£6.95 & £3.95	
Collected TV Plays Vol. 2. (A Suitable Case for Treatment, For Tea on Sunday, And Did Those Feet, The Parachute, Lets Murder Vivaldi, In Two Minds)	£6.95 & £3.95	
René de Obaldia		
Plays Vol. 1. (Jenusia *and* 7 Impromptus for Leisure)	£4.95 & £2.25	
Plays Vol. 2. (The Satyr of La Villette, The Unknown General *and* Wide Open Spaces)	£4.95	
Robert Pinget		
Plays Vol. 1. (Dead Letter, The Old Tune and Clope)	£2.25	
Plays Vol. 2. (Architruc, About Mortin *and* The Hypothesis	£4.95 & £2.25	

Nathalie Sarraute
Collected Plays (It Is There, It's Beautiful, Izzums,
   The Lie, Silence) £4.95

German Expressionism

Georg Kaiser
Plays Vol. 1. (From Morning to Midnight, The Burghers of Calais,
   The Coral, Gas I, Gas II) £6.95 & £3.50

Carl Sternehim — Plays
Scenes From the Heroic Life of the Middle Classes, The Bloomers,
   Paul Schippel, The Snob, 1913, The Fossil £6.95 & £3.50

Seven Expressionist Plays
Kokoschka, Oscar: Murderer Hope of Womankind/ Kafka,
   Franz: The Guardian of the Tomb/Barlach, Ernst: Squire
   Blue Boll/Kaiser, Georg: The Protagonist/Stramm, August:
   Awakening/Brust, Alfred: The Wolves/Goll, Ivan: Methusalem £6.95 & £3.50

Vision and Aftermath
Goering, Reinhard: *Naval Encounter*
Hasenclever, Walter: *Antigone*
Hauptmann, Carl: *A Te Deum*
Toller, Ernst: *Hinkemann* £6.95 & £3.50

Frank Wedekind
The Lulu Plays and other Sex Tragedies (Earth Spirit,
   Pandora's Box, Death and Devil, Castle Wetterstein) £6.95 & £4.50

Playscripts

John Antrobus
Trixie and Baba £3.50 & £1.95
Why Bournemouth? (*also* An Apple a Day, The Missing Links) £3.50 & £1.95

Jane Arden
Vagina Rex *and* The Gas Oven £4.50 & £1.95

Antonin Artaud
The Cenci £3.95

Howard Barker
Fair Slaughter £1.50
Stripwell *and* Claw £6.50 & £3.25
That Good Between Us (*also* Credentials of a Sympathizer) £4.95
The Love of a Good Man (*also* All Bleeding) £4.95

Stan Barstow
An Enemy of the People £1.50

Wolfgang Bauer
All Change, Party for Six, Magic Afternoon £4.95 & £2.25

Steven Berkoff
East (*also* Agamemnon, The Fall of the House of Usher) £4.95 & T.O.P.

Edward Bond
Early Morning £4.95 & £1.95

Howard Brenton and others
Lay By £4.50 & £1.95

Alan Brown
Skoolplay £1.50
Wheelchair Willie (*also* Brown Ale With Gertie, O'Connor) £5.95 & £2.95

Stewart Conn
The Aquarium (*also* The Man in the Green Muffler *and* I Didn't
   Always Live Here) £4.95 & £2.25

A.F. Cotterell
The Nutters (*also* Social Service or All Creatures Great
   and Small, *and* A Cure for All Souls) £4.50 & £1.95

Ian Curteis
Long Voyage Out of War (The Gentle Invasion, Battle at
   Trematangi, The Last Enemy) £4.95 & £1.95

Roland Dubillard
The House of Bones £4.50 & £1.95
The Swallows £3.95 & £1.95

Stanley Eveling
The Balachites, (The Strange Case of Martin Richter)   £4.50 & £1.95
Come and Be Killed,(*and* Dear Janet Rosenburg,
    Dear Mr. Koonig)   £4.50 & £1.95
The Lunatic, The Secret Sportsman, The Woman Next Door,
    and Vibrations   £4.50 & £1.95

Paul Foster
Balls (*also* Hurrah for The Bridge, The Recluse *and* The Hessian
    Corporal)   £4.50 & T.O.P.
Elizabeth 1 (*also* Satyricon *and* The Madonna in the Orchard)   £4.95 & £1.95
Heimskringla! or The Stoned Angels   £4.50 & £1.95
Marcus Brutus (*also* The Silver Queen Saloon)   £5.50 & £2.25
Tom Paine   £4.50

Tom Gallacher
Mr. Joyce Is Leaving Paris   £1.95

Peter Gill
The Sleepers Den *and* Over Gardens Out   £3.50 & £1.95

Trevor Griffiths
Occupations *and* The Big House   £3.95

Roger Howard
Slaughter Night   £3.50 & £1.95

Sandro Key-Aberg
O *and* An Empty Room   £4.50 & £1.95

Tom Mallin
Curtains   £4.50 & £1.95

Eduardo Manet
The Nuns   £4.50 & £1.95

Robert McLellan
The Hypocrite   £4.50 & £1.95

David Mowat
Anna-Luse (*also* Jens *and* Purity)   £4.50 & £1.95
The Others   £4.50 & £1.95

Obaldia, René de
Wind in the Branches of the Sassafras   £4.50 & £1.95

Pablo Picasso
Desire Caught By the Tail   £4.50 & £1.95
The Four Little Girls   £4.50 & £1.95

Jan Quackenbush
Calcium (*also* Victims *and* Once Below a Time: three plays for
    child actors including Coins, The Good Shine, Broken)   £4.50 & £1.95
Inside Out (*also* Talking of Michelangelo *and* Once Below a Time:
    three plays for child actors including Still Fires, Rolly's Grave,
    Come Tomorrow)   £3.50 & £1.95

Nathalie Sarraute
Silence *and* The Lie   £4.50 & £1.95

David Selbourne
Samson *and* Alison Mary Fagan   £4.50 & £1.95

Roland Topor
Leonardo Was Right   £1.50

Frank Wedekind
Spring Awakening   £4.95 & £1.95

Vivienne C. Welburn
Clearway   £4.50 & £1.95
Johnny So Long *and* The Drag   £4.50 & £1.95
The Treadwheel *and* Coil without Dreams   £4.95 & £2.25

Heathcote Williams
The Immortalist   £1.50
AC/DC   £4.95

Colin Wilson
Strindberg   £4.50

Snoo Wilson
Pignight *and* Blow Job   £4.95 & £2.95

Olwen Wymark
The Gymnasium (*also* The Technicians, Stay where You are,
    Jack the Giant-Killer *and* Neither Here Nor There)   £4.50 & £1.95
Three Plays (Lunchtime Concert, Coda, The Inhabitants)   £4.50